CHARLIE'S HEART

BURNING BASTARDS MC
BOOK 3

BY RYDER DANE

ISBN-10# 1-945012-05-6
ISBN-13# 978-1-945012-05-1

Edited by Vinvatar Publishing

Artwork by Jess Buffett Graphic Designs

Published by Vinvatar Publishing
Website: Vinvatar.com

TABLE OF CONTENTS

CHAPTER ONE

Charlie rode his scoot into the parking lot and parked the ancient machine next to Big Dog's bike. He wondered what the deal was tonight, Big Dog had left three messages on his cell phone, and all of them said he was needed at the clubhouse pronto.

He saw a couple of vehicles that looked like cop cars, but many of the brothers bought old cages at auction if the interceptor motors were still under the hood and customized the ugly fuckers into sweet rides that sold for a pretty profit. So it didn't overly concern him much.

He didn't want to be here, hell, he didn't want to be much of anywhere lately, at least not for a few months now. Ever since he'd let Selma fly in fact. He had always been a lobo, free from shackles and baggage. No woman could hold him for longer than a few months at a time. Those times were damn good ones, at least from his point of view, but sooner than later the females started demanding permanency, and that *was not* in his vocabulary. Until early last year, when he met Selma, she was everything he wasn't.

She was an educated woman, a lawyer in fact. She was beautiful in the way a mature woman who knew her worth was beautiful. Selma made him feel like a better man. Like he was smarter than he actually was, and she rode his prick like it was a trick pony any time, and just about anywhere the notion hit them. She was younger than he was by fourteen years, but it didn't make no never mind to either of them. She looked damned good perched on the thick cushioned bitch seat he'd bought for her little ass to sit behind him on while they enjoyed feeling the wind on their knees and the joy of freedom as the wind whipped past their cheeks.

He'd been avoiding the clubhouse, and his old pastimes held no interest for him. He had a pack of smokes in his pocket nowadays instead of his sugar packets. Why worry about dying of lung cancer if nobody was around to care anyway. He wasn't ready to hang himself, but the days after letting his lady loose, well that hanging idea hadn't seemed like such a bad notion.

She got elected to her dream job of being a circuit court judge, and he was happy for her, more happy than she probably would believe. She wanted to make a difference, and he let her go so she could. Oh she started out wanting him to continue to be part of her life, but the demands of that were too much for a man like him to concede to.

He wasn't a show horse, never had been, and when she asked him to wear a suit and tie, he'd almost laughed his ass off. Next request was to cut his hair to a more acceptable style for the image of a judge's escort to appear. He'd flatly refused both of her requests in a harsh and uncompromising way.

"I ain't no tamed whipped pup, woman, you can't rope the wind or cage a wild thing like me. I'm a biker tramp, and I ain't got no want to wear fancy clothes and sit down to dinner holding my pinky up while I have to drink some watery fuckin' tea or some shit like that."

He had regrets, but there was no way he would have missed knowing her even if he could. She was the bright spot in his life, and he was beginning to acknowledge that she'd taken a big ol' chunk of him when he'd made love to her the last time. He'd put everything he had in that last session, he wanted her to always remember him.

He walked into the club and stopped short. Big Dog was lookin' concerned, and the place was about as quiet as he'd seen since the funeral for Farley a couple of years ago. Two men in funeral suits were sitting at the table with Big Dog. Fuck, this was some kind of setup. The big man gave him a slight nod, and Charlie took a couple of moments to center himself. He hated fuckin' cops.

Tiny handed him a beer as he walked by, and he nodded to the man in thanks, and kept on moving. He stood behind the suits and said, "Hey, Big D, what's going on?"

The two men tried to crane their necks to see the man they'd come to see, but the prez waved him into a chair on his right side. Charlie hesitated for a few heartbeats and sat down. No one spoke. He didn't like the way the cross-eyed fuckers were staring at him. He drained his beer and slowly placed it on the table in front of him before folding his hands and looking directly at the bigger of the two men.

"Okay, I'm here, there must be a reason for this unsolicited visit. Let's get on with you tellin' me what you think you can accuse me of doing, and I'll deny it. Go ahead, I'm not in a bad mood or nothin'."

The two glanced at each other and the short one nodded. "You are Charles Vernon?" Charlie nodded, not bothering to answer verbally, what would be the point?

"I'm Agent Hill, and this is my partner Agent Scott. We're here to ask you a few questions about a woman that we believe you know." He opened the file in front of him and passed over a glossy eight by ten of Selma. Seeing her made his guts tighten, but outwardly he nodded.

"Yeah, I know her, she's a good woman and a fair judge." Seeing the agent fingering the file, he got a tingle up his spine. "Why dontcha just come out with it? I need another beer, but since I don't drink with strangers and people I don't trust. I have to wait till you're done beatin' around the fuckin' bush. Is there a problem with me being her friend?"

Both agents shook their heads and looked at Big Dog before continuing. He shrugged his shoulders and folded his hands across his belly as he continued to lounge in the chair.

Agent Hill cleared his throat and sighed. He blew out his breath and blurted it out. "The Honorable Judge Selma Pearson has disappeared, and we have reason to believe her life is in danger."

Agent Scott took up the conversation from there. "Judge Pearson was last seen on Friday, January twenty-ninth. She has been missing since approximately eight thirty pm. If you have been keeping up with the news during the past year, you would know that the area has had three high profile child endangerment, and abuse neglect cases.

"Two weeks before her disappearance, she began getting threats, at first they came through the switchboard at the courthouse, then the threats were sent by mail. One such letter demanded the writer's children be returned to them or she would pay for taking the children. The problem here is that we have three names of families that could be behind this entire thing. All of the cases were related in that the cousins and aunts and uncles were all from the same clan of people and all of them deny any knowledge."

At first Charlie felt poleaxed, Selma was missing? His woman was probably in the hands of people cruel enough that their children had been removed from the homes? He shook his head at the picture that was conjured in his brain. "Who has her?" The Agents both shrugged their shoulders.

"Mr. Vernon, I'm afraid we cannot tell you the names of the families, we came here because of the judge's phone records. We had a small hope that she was with you because of the many phone calls she has made to your cell phone in the last two weeks, and she has called your number at least twenty times during the past months before that. We have to search out every clue, sir. It appears we have drawn the wrong conclusion concerning your relationship."

Charlie stood before they could move from their seats. "I asked you for a name, I don't give a shit what you think about anything." His voice was low and deadly as he put his fingertips on the table. "I asked you nicely once, I won't ask again and you fuckers better get ready for an asswhippin' if you're gonna protect the people holding my woman."

Big Dog intervened by snatching the folder from in front of Agent Hill. "Cool your shit, gentlemen, you won't make it out of the room without giving us a name, this way, you are not culpable if someone was to find out who you suspect right? The folder fell open on the table and someone might have seen your list of suspects, simple and non-violent. Ah, well I'll be a motherfucker, there's a few names we've heard of before. You boys better take some heavy firepower with you when you go into them hills. Those people are a different breed of human."

He slid the folder back toward the agents, with the cover open where Charlie could see the information he wanted. "Thank you for stopping by and we hope you find the judge real soon. She has friends here at the club, and if the Burning Bastards can help you in any way, we'll be sure and let you know what we find."

The agents were at least smart enough to know they had been dismissed, and Preacher escorted them to the door, watching to make certain they left the grounds safely, with no detours.

Behind him in the room, Big Dog and Charlie had the table they had been sitting at flipped up to check for listening devices. The table was clean, but the chair Agent Scott had been sitting in had a small black disc adhered to the underside. Big Dog grinned and took the chair outside & set it next to his Harley. He started the motor and revved it several times just to fuck with the agents. The laughter coming from the men that came out of the building lightened the mood for a few minutes.

Agent Hill's chair was clean, but it was taken outside too. Preacher began quoting scripture when Big Dog shut down the powerful engine and walked back to the door of the club.

He made a detour when he saw Charlie walk around the corner of the building with his cell phone in hand. He hesitated to disturb the greybeard, but Charlie was listening to the receiver and yanking on his hair at the same time. He finally closed the old cell, and from the way the older man's shoulders slumped forward, Big Dog couldn't help but make his presence known.

"Hey, what's going on?"

Charlie didn't want to talk, he wanted to eat his .45. "I swore I wouldn't bother her again, I swore I wouldn't pick up the fuckin' phone when she called. She kept calling, Big Dog, she kept calling me for help and I was too fuckin' thick headed to pick up the goddamned phone. She needed me and I fuckin' let her down."

Big Dog looked at his old friend with pity. "Charlie, if you can hang on for a few I'll call a few of the guys to go with you, or I can call Future and let her know I'll be late. You should have company on the trip."

Charlie shook his grey head, "No, I know the people that have her. Old Birdsong has a bad case of isolationism. I don't dare bring anyone with me. That fucker would start shooting before he ever asked for a name."

He slapped the prez on his arm, "It'll be fine, if things go well, I might even bring you back a quart of the best shine you ever tasted. I should be back in a week or two, much over that and you can give my stuff to Pressley."

He nodded again and started walking to his bike. The old sled never failed to soothe his torment in the past, and he hoped he could count on the same healing tonight. He had to think, and the agent's words about her disappearing from the area hit him, nothing prepared him to hear her begging him to come and save her from the people before they took her.

"Please, Daddy, you said you'd always be there if I needed you, I need you. I am so afraid. Please answer the phone."

"I guess you were just saying the words you thought I wanted to hear. If you really loved me you would be here."

"Birdsong and Juanita won't stop. They have been driving past my place over and over, I don't dare turn on my lights at night. The police are patrolling more, but they seem to know when the cops aren't around. They want the kids back, but, Charlie, I swear, those children were in such bad shape that I couldn't send them back. We had to send the kids out of the area because their parents tried to kidnap them from the hospital."

"I wish you were here to talk to, this job is great, but I had to trade the man I love, and my best friend, to get it. Oh yeah, I bought a gun, I just hope I have the guts to pull the trigger if I need to."

A few of the messages were random thoughts, like she was either drunk or sleep deprived. His bet would be sleep deprivation. His mailbox was full, so he deleted five of the more inane messages, just in case she could call him if she got the chance.

Charlie knew who Birdsong and Juanita were. He'd bought a few quarts of grade A shine from the man, and a leather pelt cover for his sled's seat a few years back.

Birdsong Johnson was a hill country man with a serious case of mean. He ran a corn liquor still, and shot at anyone who showed up close to his homestead. How in the hell the authorities got their hands on the kids had to be a miracle because those hill folk were not the kind of people that believed in education.

Charlie could only imagine the case of mad Birdsong had going on with the fact a split tail judge had taken his kids away. It would have been bad enough for a male judge, but a female, well that would have gone straight to the old boy's pride.

Juanita Johnson was the most browbeaten woman Charlie had ever seen. She must've whelped her first born around fourteen years old. She was the daughter of another hill country family. The last time he'd seen her she still looked too young to have three brats hanging on her skirts. That had been a few years ago. Who knew how many kids were in the litter by now.

The first thing he needed to do was to go home and get some cash, old Birdsong didn't take plastic, and Charlie understood the man's refusal to negotiate prices for his product. Thankfully he'd been a customer before so it wouldn't look suspicious when he showed up.

He left the Indian at the bottom of the wooded hills and shrugged on his camping gear. It took a while for the old familiar cadence of moving without thinking, one foot in front of the other, to give him a sense of peace. His attention was on the woods and downed logs as he went deeper into the inclining landscape.

He'd changed his plans from showing up to purchase some of Birdsong's moonshine, mainly due to the fact he had time to think about what a man used to secrecy would do if he had kidnapped someone important.

He could have rode the scoot up on the two track that passed for a road to the enclave where the clan lived, but he knew the mentality of Birdsong, Selma wouldn't be kept at the homestead for the authorities to find so easily. Strangers, even familiar strangers, would never know there was a kidnap victim nearby, and no one but Birdsong himself would speak to visitors.

It was a hell of a climb, and Charlie cursed himself for allowing his body to go soft like it had. He'd exchanged the pack of smokes for a baggie of sugar packets, not only for his health, but he didn't need to alert one of the Johnson clan that someone was on their hill by letting the cigarette smoke reach their noses. The side benefit was the extra energy he would need to navigate through the dense woods. He was the victim of low blood sugar, instead of shots to keep his sugar at an acceptable level, he was forced to eat high protein and carbohydrates, it was a good thing they made those little packets of peanut butter crackers, or he would starve to death nowadays.

Thinking about his eating habits just brought his mood further down. Once Selma found out about his issue, she cooked regularly for the two of them. When he left her, his nutrition had gone to shit. Why should he bother to care, he didn't answer to anyone, *dammit*.

It was almost full dark by the time he decided that he wouldn't get any further without breaking an ankle in the dark. He didn't bother to light a fire, or even pitch his tent tonight. His bedroll would be sufficient for his needs, and he remembered to take the painkillers for his arthritic knees so he'd be able to walk the next day.

It took a long time for him to doze off, and even then his sleep wasn't restful, his mind continually replayed her messages that she'd left on his phone. "You said you would always be there if I needed you. Daddy, I'm scared, please, please, pick up the phone, or call me back."

CHAPTER TWO

She'd done everything she could think of to hide from the Johnson clan. She knew she had to stop crying over the fact Charlie refused to answer her calls and he probably had moved on in the past months since they'd last been together.

She hung up the connection when the automated voice told her the voice mailbox she was trying to connect with was full.

He had been her only real hope at keeping her safe, and now she cried ugly tears of fear and betrayal. She would have bet her life that Charlie meant what he told her before he left the bed they'd shared and made love in most of the night before.

"If you ever need me, you call and I'll be there. I've never told a woman that I loved her like I love you, but you need to follow your dreams, girl, and I'm not the kind of man you need by your side while you're livin' those dreams."

He'd wiped the tears from her cheeks with his big thumb and licked the liquid off. "I don't want to be the cause of your tears, girl, a man shouldn't make his woman cry hurtful tears, and if I stick around you will cry later on when you realize being with me is holding you from getting elected. I wouldn't be able to look in a mirror to shave or comb my damn hair if I was to be the reason your dream couldn't come true."

Election night she'd come home to find a dozen yellow roses and one blood red one in the center with a card that said, "Proud of you, and may all of your dreams come true."

He hadn't signed the card, but she knew who sent the beautiful flowers, and she'd sat at her kitchen table and bawled her eyes out that night. It was so unfair, and she hated the job that she loved because she couldn't have it all like she'd always believed a woman could. She could have the dream, or she could have the man of her dreams, one or the other, and it sucked.

Now she needed him to hold her in his strong arms and tell her everything would be all right, but he had cut the tie between them, and she was alone. She fell asleep on the sofa they'd first made love on, and woke up to see Birdsong Johnson staring at her.

She opened her mouth to scream and she saw the raised fist that she hadn't ducked fast enough to avoid.

She woke up when she was pulled from under the backseat of a vehicle that she didn't recognize. She realized then that someone else must have been driving Birdsong's old pick-up as a decoy for the police to be looking out for.

Juanita stared at her in fear, but Selma kept her eyes on the gruff wiry man. He could use a good scrubbing from the smell of the him, and he grinned at her with tobacco stained rotting teeth. She wanted to put her fingers to her jaw to see if anything was broken, but her upper arms were taped to her sides, and she couldn't get her hand up far enough to touch her face.

"You thought you'd get away with takin' my kids, but you gonna learn a lesson, girly, they give 'em back, they get you back." He looked her up and down with disgust, and shook his head as if he'd found her unattractive. "While you're at it, you're gonna tell me how you got the little fuckers off of my property, I ain't a patient man, so you need to talk."

Selma wasn't about to divulge anything to this man and she knew he wouldn't like it. There was no way for her to brace herself from the fist upside her head again. Her jaw still hurt from the last time he'd hit her, and she screamed and spat the blood from her mouth at his feet.

Her jerked her back to her feet and spat tobacco juice over his shoulder before grabbing her arm and dragging her toward the woods.

"I gave you the chance to tell me what I want to know, but you split tails are all alike, a bunch of lyin', connivin' whores. So I'm takin' you to your new home. You ain't used to a place like this one, but it's what happens when you steal from a man, an' mess with his family."

They walked for what seemed like miles to her. Her feet were a mess of cuts and she felt the liquid of her bloody scrapes trickle through her toes as she was towed along. Finally they came to a cave of sorts dug into the side of a small hill, and Selma knew this would be her prison. She pulled back when Birdsong kept walking toward the hole in the side of the hill.

"No, please don't do this, you are already wanted by the police for what you did to your children, what makes you think they will give the children back to live in the same situation? You allowed men to fondle your ten-year-old daughter for God's sake. You hit your twelve-year-old so hard he is deaf and blind on the right side of his head. The others are in bad shape too. Why are you doing this?"

He ignored her words and she dug her bloody heels into the rotted leaves, but it caused her to skate and fall into a position of almost the splits. *Fuck that hurt*. Her hamstrings were screaming bloody murder, but the sound of Birdsong laughing maniacally brought her attention back to him.

"Stupid bitch, my eyes are blue, Juanita's eyes are blue, Oona, her eyes are brown, she ain't my kid, neither is Corbin, and two of the other youngins. Winters up here are cold and a single man has needs, for the right price a man might let his friends take their ease between the thighs of his property. God makes his choice whether to plant a stranger's seed or not. I ain't gonna argue with the almighty."

He yanked her wrist and she screamed as she felt the bone in her shoulder pop and separate from its socket. He kept towing her and dragged her inside the dirt cave. In the middle of the floor, was a new patch of concrete with a heavy logging chain embedded in the hardened square that was eight foot long with a round metal shackle welded to the end of the chain.

"Oh hell no, you can't do this to me." She kicked her feet at him and connected to his knee, but he grunted and gave her a kick in the thigh.

"Stupid bitch, you're lucky I plan to make you live for a while, and if you learn, after the hunt is over for you, I'll let you live until you step outta line." He bent down to grab her now useless leg by the ankle and jerked it toward his other hand that held the metal circlet. He patted her knee once he'd secured the thick padlock holding the two metal halves together. He grinned at her again and chuckled.

"I figure it this ways, if you make it out of this dug out alive, it will be cold an' frosty by the time they stop huntin' for you. I can make a pretty penny off selling the chance to fuck a split tail judge. I'll be able to sell your services to the highest bidder and if they pay enough, or they have to pool their money and fuck you all together, it makes me no never mind cause the next men'll step right up to ream your ass out for all the indignities men have to put up with. Don't that idea make your cunt just wetter than a heifer in heat?"

He laughed, and left her sitting in the dirt.

It was getting dark outside, and from the meager light coming through the open mouth of her prison, she got on all fours and did a crab side crawl to the low table which was actually planks lying on top of round pieces of firewood, where she spied a blanket.

The crawl was painful and she had to gasp for breath a few times as she hauled herself onto the planks to get her body up off the damp earth. There was only one other person on earth who knew she had a deathly fear of bugs, and he was nowhere nearby to kill them or brush them away from her skin.

She screamed when she shook the blanket out and two mice jumped from the folds of the material where they had begun building their nest.

Crying was counterproductive, but there was nothing else to do, "I will be strong again tomorrow, tonight I will forgive myself for being weak. Tomorrow I can face the fact I'm the only one I can rely on. Ha, maybe if I cry loud enough the bears will stay away."

She resented the job that she loved. "Oh sure, you are a big time judge, and look where it has gotten you, Selma, old girl." She looked around in the dark as pitch hole in the ground and shook her head. "Yes indeed, you could have been in your own bed with the only man who ever truly gave a damn enough about you to leave rather than be an embarrassment to you.

"You are getting exactly what you deserved, he moved on and you let him go." She thought for a minute and narrowed her eyes in the darkness. "Oh no, when I get out of here I will drag his ass kicking and screaming with me, if the voters can't accept him then they don't need me either. I can still practice law, fuck this, Charles Vernon, look out, Hurricane Selma is going to lock your handsome ass down, and I'm going to make you like it dammit!"

She dreamed that Charlie was looking for her, and she kept calling for him to help her, but she woke abruptly when she rolled off the planks and landed on her dislocated shoulder. The bone shoved itself back into place, and her screams made her own ears hurt from the pain she's experienced as she felt it pop back into the socket.

When she could breathe without gasping for air, she grabbed a handful of dirt and threw it as hard as she could into the darkness. The frustrated scream that left her mouth helped her to center herself. Her arm was still basically useless, but it should be better in a few days, as long as the bastard kept his hands to himself.

His threats to sell her wares made her shudder, but she would not give into the despair. If she had to, she would defend herself, at least now that she had something to use as a weapon. The long branches at the mouth of her cave would make a decent weapon, as long as her chain was long enough to get close enough to pull one of the dead saplings inside the hole with her so she could trim it down and strip it of the smaller branches and leaves.

Once daylight came, she would be able to scope out her domain and she would have a better idea of what her options might be. She crawled back onto her plank bed and closed her eyes. "Charlie, Daddy, I am so sorry, I love you, please find me before it's too late."

CHAPTER THREE

Each morning Selma woke and used the two foot deep hole in the corner of the room to take care of her bodily functions. It was gross and disgusting, but it was better than nothing. There were two two-gallon jugs filled with potable water for which she was thankful, and there were several cans of food too. Nothing that could be considered an actual meal, but her appetite was almost nil anyway. She still forced herself to eat something each day. If the opportunity came for her to escape, she would be alert and have energy to run.

On the forth morning she woke to the low sound of voices coming toward her cave. She stepped close enough to the side wall and craned her neck trying to see who was coming to visit. Her heart sank when she saw it was only Birdsong and his wife, so she walked back to her wooden bed and sat down.

Juanita walked into the cave and hesitated before coming closer to the docile prisoner.

"I done brought you some food an' some more water. You better get used to your own company, I cain't be bothered coming up here an' babysittin' your ass. I got chores to do, an' now that you took my kids, their chores fall on my shoulders. It ain't right that you should take a momma's children like you did."

All the while Juanita was talking tough she looked at Selma with gratitude and pleading.

Her head jerked to the side to let the judge who helped get her children away from the monster she was stuck living with. The big van had pulled into the yard, and she'd handed the baby to the judge personally, and so far she hadn't been sorry that her kids now had a chance to have a life away from this place. She would do whatever she could to help the woman who liberated the kids, but there wasn't much she could do yet.

She leaned in close and told Selma, "Sorry, ma'am, but could you squeak or yell a little bit, like maybe I was slappin' you?"

The younger woman was good, she slapped her own arm and Selma let out a scream that brought a smile and a nod from Juanita.

"You took my kids, how did you get them? Who helped you?" Another skin on skin slap and Selma continued to do her best to let out convincing noises of pain.

"You'd best tell me, 'cause Birdsong's cousin's kids was took that same day and we want our kids back."

All the while she was leaning near Selma asking if the kids were okay. She was reassured by the direct eye contact and nod.

"I'm tryin' to figure a way to let you get loose without Birdsong knowin' it was me."

After the last slap and scream, Selma told her in a slightly raised voice, "I wasn't involved in acquiring the children, social services brought the children into the courtroom and the doctor reports on their conditions. None of them have even had a vaccination, six of the thirteen children have serious mental health challenges ahead of them and need to go into special foster homes that are trained to deal with their unique issues. If you loved your children as much as you say you do, then you would have protected them and sent them to school.

"I am a judge, I believe in and follow the law, when I see children that have been abused to the point yours were, you're damn right I signed the papers removing your parental rights."

She knew that she'd pushed too far when she heard the fast shuffle of booted feet heading their way, and she nodded to Juanita. The woman had tears in her eyes when she drew back her hand and slapped Selma in the face, hard. She allowed herself to fall sideways to the dirt, and pretended to be barely conscious for the benefit of Birdsong's intense stare.

He stood over her and pointed a stained finger at her. "You just signed your own trip to hell, bitch. Nobody talks to me or mine like that. You better hope the water and food here last a good long time, 'cause you're gonna die right here. Once you're dead, I'll jest cover the hole and forget you. Juanita ain't comin' back with a damn thing to keep you alive. You gonna have time to think about trespassin' on this family, but you'll be dead in a week."

She didn't bother to say anything as the evil bastard towed Juanita from the cave, leaving her alone once again.

She pushed herself back into a sitting position. If she heard him right, he planned to leave her to die of exposure or starvation. "Okay, Selma, there is a bright side to this, at least you won't be used as a prostitute, Hillbilly style or not." The knowledge made her laugh in a slightly hysterical way, but laughing served its purpose in allowing some of the stress of her situation leave her mind.

Charlie woke slowly. Every fucking muscle appeared to be screaming at him, and he groaned. "You outta shape, fucker, shit man."

He used the tree behind him to pull himself to a standing position. His thighs felt like they were on fire and his lower back was one big pain. He made it three steps away from where he'd slept before needing to take a leak. Once that was taken care of he felt a little better, but kept cursing his laziness over the past few years.

He dug a granola bar and a bottle of water from his pack to get his blood sugar back up so he'd have energy to move today. He thought about the climb that would be on today's agenda and groaned again.

"Ya dumb fuck, always needin' to do shit the hard way. You should've told Big Dog to hop on his scoot and gather a few more brothers to rescue Selma, but no, you gotta be fuckin' Superman or some shit."

Thinking of Selma made his cock twitch and he shook his head. "The only fuckin' muscle that don't hurt, well hell, at least I ain't so old I need a goddamned pill to get it to work. Go to sleep you horny fuck. She ain't gonna be in any shape for what you want for a while, if she'll ever want me again after this."

It took most of the morning for him to reach the top of the hill. The hilltop was bare of trees and only had minimal ground cover, and he cursed his bad luck, but dropped his pack twenty feet before he reached the crest while crawling on his belly. By the date the cops had said she was taken until now, Selma had been in Birdsong's possession for seven days. Who knew what kind of shit that old hillbilly had done to her.

He remembered the fading bruises that he'd seen on Juanita's face the day he'd been there before, and the thought that Birdsong might have hurt her enraged him. "That fucker better not have touched her in a harmful way." He knew in his mind Selma hadn't been treated delicately and finally felt his old skill come over his mind. First get her to safety, then deal with her captor. If Birdsong was in his way to reach her...

He would be eliminated where he stood.

He used the scope on his rifle to recon the area of the hollow of the Johnson homestead. The place looked deserted, but Charlie knew better than to think he could just walk down into the place without worrying about a cap being put in his back.

A few people that were reported as lost in this area, were never found. Until Selma was safe, he would remain cautious. Afterwards, well that would depend on the damage she suffered.

Charlie spied Juanita sneaking around the backside of the house and it looked like she began to head east. She suddenly stopped in her tracks and turned around to run back to the house.

He trained the sight toward the east of the wooden house and took his time scanning the terrain for any telltale hint of a shed or shelter where they might have his woman hidden away.

There was movement from the house, and he redirected his sight to the person moving around on the porch. Ol' Birdsong was carrying a long gun and Juanita came out of the house behind him with her dress clutched in front of her body. He watched Birdsong backhand the small woman and knock her to the planked floor of the porch. She stayed down, and Charlie figured that was probably the smartest thing for her to do at the time. The shine maker left off the steps and headed east.

This was too much of a coincidence for Charlie. He did a quick scan to make sure no one was near enough to be spying him as he backed slowly from his spot on top of the hill and grabbed his pack and double stepped it east. He hated to feel his guts were twisting, that always happened when trouble of the physical variety began. He knew with everything inside that he was going to kill Birdsong one way or the other. The man would never get another shot at Selma.

He was ahead of Birdsong and slowly crept down the hill behind scrub bushes and briars. As he made his way down, he scanned the area around him and his eyes lit on a hole in the side of the hill. "Fuck, he's gonna' be a goddamned pleasure to kill."

Sure enough, the walking dead man came into his sight and Charlie waited impatiently for the fucker to step into the cavern. He followed slowly and heard the bastard laughing as he taunted someone.

There was the sound of something hitting what sounded like flesh and Charlie rounded the corner of the cave to see Selma standing with a small log in her hand and Birdsong bending over to pick up the gun from the floor.

It was time for Charlie to intervene, the bigger man was pissed off that the woman had knocked his gun from his hand and he cussed a blue streak as Charlie stepped up behind him.

"Hey, Birdsong, I have a bone to pick with you, motherfucker."

His first word had the big man turn his head toward the newcomer and Charlie's boot connected with his jaw. He looked up at *his woman* and saw her back away, still clutching her weapon to her chest. She looked wild and dirty as hell but she was alive and he smiled at her before squaring off with Birdsong again.

"You should've never touched what's mine you dumbfuck, what in the hell did you think would happen when you steal a man's woman?"

Birdsong shook his hard head and asked Charlie, "What the fuck are you talkin' 'bout? This split tail? She took the kids from the families up here, what would you've done if some high and mighty whore did that to you? Hey, ain't you that biker fuck from a few years ago? What the hell, man, we can finish this matter later, and I got a new batch of some of the best fuckin' shine ready to sell right up at the house."

A small rock, followed by another rock pelted Birdsong on his shoulder and he redirected his gaze to Selma.

Charlie grinned at his girl, she hadn't lost her fire. "Babydoll, Birdsong and me, we're just dancing a bit darlin', I'll be with you directly and get you back to where you belong. Hang on, okay?"

She answered with a stone to the chest that stung even through the thin t-shirt he was wearing. "Hurry up, I am sick of the place, accommodations here suck."

Charlie gave a shout of laughter and nodded at her, before turning to Birdsong. "You heard her, time to die." The fist hit his jaw and the fight was on.

All through the fight Charlie kept cursing his lazy habits in the past few years. The fact Birdsong was a few inches taller and quite a few pounds heavier didn't matter. Charlie felt every punch and kick, he hoped Birdsong felt his hits at least as hard. If he made it out of this day alive, he was going to start joining the brothers in the weight room again, fuck this shit.

The bigger man made a grave mistake when he reached down in the top of his boot and pulled a pig sticker. One thing Charlie was damn fuckin' good at was knives and he pulled his own knife. "You know, I wasn't sure there for a minute I was going to win this fight honorable like, now I see I don't have to worry about that, do I?"

Birdsong crouched, ready to shuffle and jab, but Charlie wanted this day over with and sent his balanced blade straight into his enemy's throat hard enough for the tip to be seen sticking from the flesh on the opposite side of the man's neck. The wound didn't stop the man's momentum and he moved forward faster than Charlie could get far enough away from the glancing slice along the top of his rib.

What made Charlie look toward Selma with surprise was the piece of wood she'd been using as a club earlier, sailed with enough force to shove Birdsong's face back when it hit right between his eyes.

The screech that came from his lady peeled the skin from his ears, but he was so happy to see that she wasn't layin' in a puddle of tears that he grinned and forgot his wound while he went to her to give her the hug he needed.

The closer he got to her, the more he could see the wild, desperate look on her face, and the tears sliding through the dirt on her face. She was shaking in fine tremors and he looked back over his shoulder wondering if it would be stupid if he carved the fucker up some.

"Hey, babydoll, I see you can still hit what you aim at." He slowed his steps because she didn't acknowledge him at all. Shit, she was shocky and he didn't have a damn thing with him to help her but a warm embrace, so he didn't give her time to punch him, he reached for her and drew her into his arms, holding her tight to his chest.

She didn't struggle, but she didn't return his hug right away either. He choked up like a damn woman, but she was breaking his heart here. He had to clear his throat a couple of times before he could speak and not bawl like a titty baby.

"I was so worried about you, girl, you got no idea how much I'm sorry I didn't pick up the phone when you called. I'm a stubborn old fool, and I don't deserve for you to forgive me, but I'll do anything for you. I heard your voice and you sounded so scared, I wasn't with you."

He loosened one arm and held her jaw in his hand so he could see her face. "I love you, babydoll, you can believe that, even if you don't have faith in anything else. I came as

33

soon as I could and it wasn't fast enough. I'm sorry, baby, so sorry."

CHAPTER FOUR

Selma heard someone coming and knew Birdsong would be checking on her to see if she was still alive. She picked up the foot long section of firewood and held it to her side as she stood waiting for her captor to show his filthy ass. She was tired, she was scared, and she was cornered. She had nothing to lose if she fought back, and she planned to fight for her life.

She had been here alone for the past three days and nights, but the only time it actually bothered her was at nighttime, when the predators became curious and she would see only the glint of a yellow or green set of eyes in the darkness. She chucked rocks and empty jars that had held the preserved food she'd been eating. So far the animals had left after she began screaming at them to go away in the darkness.

When Birdsong rounded the short corner, she'd brought the wood down onto his fingers holding the rifle, and watched the weapon fall from his grasp. She was raising the wood to her shoulder when she noticed the shadow slowly coming up behind the cursing man who bent down to pick up the gun.

Hearing Charlie's voice stunned her. Her heart thumped hard in her chest and she backed away when he smiled at her and kicked the bigger man in the jaw. All she could think was that *he'd come to save her.* Charlie was here, he kept his promise, and while she didn't register most of what he said to Birdsong, his words, "My Woman" warmed her deep inside. She wasn't alone now, her love came for her, claimed her, and was fighting her enemy to rescue her.

She saw the knife in Birdsong's hand slice through Charlie's shirt and didn't stop to think when she threw the chunk of wood in her hand at his head. Nobody was going to hurt her man without dealing with her.

Seeing that a knife stuck through the big man's throat stopped her from grabbing another piece of wood and attacking him. He hit the ground and she ignored him as Charlie approached her cautiously. She let go of her fear as he held her to his strong chest. His heart was beating hard under her cheek, and she felt so safe being enclosed in his tight embrace, that she never wanted to move from this spot with him.

She heard him calling her babydoll, and her arms closed tight around his slender waist. His big hand holding her swollen jaw so tenderly gave her hope. "Charlie, I prayed you would come, and here you are, I knew you would come."

That was all she said as she slumped in his arms, passed out from exhaustion, and the release of fear.

"Oh hell, woman, this is a bad place for you to take a nap, but if that's what you want to do, we'll stay right here 'till you wake up. Seeing how he treated you like a damned animal makes me want to feed him to the fuckin' cougars and wild boar."

He gently lowered her slight form to the dirty blanket covered pallet and went to search Birdsong's pockets for the key to the padlock holding the leg shackle in place. He had to roll the big man over to go through his pockets, and left everything he found on the ground next to the body. The fucker had a leather thong with several keys on it and Charlie grabbed it up. He had some difficulty pulling his knife free, but a boot to the side of the bastards head helped his efforts and he wiped his blade on the dead man's shirt. He stabbed the blade into the dirt to the hilt a few times to clean the red off better before sliding it back into his boot.

He heard a noise and reached for his knife again, but he saw Juanita standing at the mouth of the cave and she was peeking inside.

"You might as well come inside, I hope you don't put me to the trouble of chasing you down. I don't hurt women, even one's married to the likes of this fucker." He turned his back on her, took the keys to where Selma was tethered, and began trying out the keys one by one.

"All I want is to get my woman off this hill and to a safe place."

He felt her move closer and glanced up at the key dangling from Juanita's fingertips. He nodded, and took the keys to unlock the metal from her ankle. Seeing the condition of her dainty feet, made him realize she wasn't walking out of this place on her own.

"Mr., I was coming to let her loose, you don't have to worry none, the judge here did me a favor by takin' the kids, and I owe her for not tellin' Birdsong that I was the one to call the social workers. I want to help her."

Charlie could see the woman shaking, she kept glancing at her husband's body and looking back at Selma. She wouldn't look at him directly, and he figured it was probably fear that held her tight.

"You want to help the judge here, I appreciate that, but unless you have someway for me to carry her off of this hill, we will be stuck here until I can get some brothers up here to help. I can carry her, God knows I would try, but I won't get her back over the hill before my people can get here. So unless you have another way to take us to my scoot, we'll be your guests."

Juanita appeared to be thinking, and she smiled for the first time that he'd ever seen.

"There should be a key to the car they brung her here in on that leather, Ol' Merl and Saul took the truck to go buy sugar and provisions, the car belongs to Merl. I can take you to your motorbike I guess, they'll be here by mornin' so I can't take you to town an' be back here pretendin' to worry about Birdsong."

He bent down to pick up his ladylove, and started walking to the cave's entrance.

Juanita hung back for a few minutes, and ran past him once she'd lit the fuze on the sticks of dynamite that she put under Birdsong's fat belly. She'd grabbed the cash and left him lie.

"You might want to speed it up a bit, I don't know how old those sticks of dynamite is, but they was startin' to leak when I took them outta the sack." She kept going and Charlie looked around for cover.

They were only about fifty feet from the cave, and his knees weren't up to running right now, even if he wasn't carrying the extra weight. He crouched down and laid Selma's unconscious body on the soft ground cover, before lying on top of her, covering her face and torso from flying rocks and debris. He tried to keep his weight off her chest, but the impact of the explosion shoved him down on top of her hard. He was so stunned by the impact of rocks that pelted his head and back, that it took a few minutes for him to realize what he was doing, and he pushed himself from her body.

He sat up and had to orient himself for a few long minutes. The last explosion that big he'd been around for was in Nam, and the results of that had been a titanium plate in his head and several years of riding his bike to help him settle his past experiences. He kept his eyes trained on Selma, if he closed them he knew he would see the movie running through his brain of that last mission. He didn't want to see that again. Seeing body parts flying around you, well, it had a big impact on his life. Her eyes fluttered open and he leaned down to kiss her.

She chased his demons away. Once they became lovers, his nightmares were almost gone. She'd been his touchstone, and there was no way he would let her go again, somehow, some way, he would find a way for them to be together.

She was waking up and he pushed her hair back from her face with a shaking hand. Fuck, he couldn't lose her again. He got to his feet and pulled her up and into his arms to resume the walk to the Johnson homestead. Nothing mattered but the woman in his arms. He ignored the way the almost non-existent cartilage in his knees stabbed pain through his thighs and kept putting one foot in front of the other.

He left Selma in the house with Juanita while he got a drink, and headed back to the hill to retrieve his rifle and pack. He thought about leaving them, but that rifle had kept him alive many times over, and he'd be damned if he would leave it to be ruined in this place. The three long swallows of good corn liquor had helped oil his joints, and dull the pain so this walk wasn't bad.

Seeing the hole in the hillside made him whistle. He wondered how many sticks of the dynamite she used, because half of the hill resembled a molehill. There was no sign of

Birdsong, and that was all to the good. He found his things and went back to the house.

It was time to take his woman home.

Hearing Juanita helping Selma around upstairs, Charlie headed to the bathroom where they were and walked in while they were talking. He noticed Juanita had helped her to the bathroom and given her a washcloth to wash her face and arms. He hated to break up the hen party. "I hate to break into this reunion, but we need to get moving if we plan on getting off this hill before dark."

All the way down the hill, Juanita kept telling Selma about the kids and how she worried about them. "I know you'll give them good homes and plenty of food, but I'm still gonna worry 'bout them. You promised you'd send for me if they need me, so I'll be holding you to your word."

They were finally at the bottom of the hill close to where he'd parked his bike and he wanted to get moving. Juanita started the old car and jumped back out to give Selma a hug, and crooked her fingers at him to come to the vehicle. *Fuck, now what*?

She pulled the bungee cord loose from the trunk and opened it to reveal five cases of quart jars filled with Birdsong's moonshine. "Here you go Mr., you take whatever you can carry. I plan to run the still now, and anytime you want more, you just come back, and you can have a few quarts anytime you want them." She leaned down when he bent to select a couple of quarts, and said, "You take good care of that woman now, you hear me? She's a saint." She grabbed two more quarts and followed him back to the scoot.

He put the four quarts in his saddlebags and hoped they didn't crack and leak out, but Juanita ran back to the car and came back with two old pieces of cloth to wrap them in.

"There you go. Judge, don't forget, you promised, and I'll be content knowing my babies are getting what they need."

She left them there and Charlie smiled at Selma. He had to step up to her and hold her one more time before they got on the Indian and got back to town. She squeezed his ribs tight as they kissed.

"We're going to sort us out as soon as I get this mess about the children straightened out. I am serious, we have to find a way, I can't keep living without you."

He nodded his head. "Goes both ways, babydoll, now, let's get situated and get out of here." He got one more kiss and backed the bike out of the bushes completely and onto the road.

Once he reached the main road, he gave the throttle a twist, and the old bike ate up the miles. It occurred to him that they were exactly where they should be, on the bike, with her arms around his waist holding him tight. He gave a shout of sheer happiness and got an extra hard squeeze from behind him. *Fuckin' A there would be some way, it was just fucking hair.*

As much as he wanted to, he didn't take her home. He stopped the bike at the emergency room entrance of the hospital, and cut the engine.

"Don't leave me, Daddy, you can get your cuts taken care of and be with me, can't you?" She hated hearing the desperation in her voice, but she couldn't let him walk away, she needed him. "You promise you'll come in with me, or I won't go inside, I mean it."

He was weary to the bone, but wasn't ready to let her stray too far from his sight either. "Babydoll, I'll stay with you as long as they let me, but we both know they are gonna have questions that we won't be answering the same. They are gonna at least take me in to question me, and probably lock me up until the suits bail my ass out. I killed a man, and it don't matter what walk of life or what he's done. He's dead."

She grabbed his arm and shook it. "Birdsong Johnson died tragically in an explosion when he tried to kill me. You pulled me from the cave just before the place went up with Birdsong inside. That is what I saw, and that is what they will hear from me. You were just arriving when you saw him put the dynamite down and you ran inside to get me out. They won't arrest my hero. I won't let them. Do you understand what I am saying?

Birdsong died a deserved death, and you might have wanted to kill him, but you didn't."

He pulled her close and kissed her again before letting her go so he could go inside for a wheelchair. It would be a miracle if the cops believed her story, but he trusted her word, and resigned himself to being henpecked.

CHAPTER FIVE

In the end, her story was taken as the official record of happenings. Charlie's injuries supported the story, and Charlie knew she wasn't happy the doctor at the hospital declared that she was dehydrated and had signs of mild exposure, her feet had several stones and briars embedded under the skin. He said she would need to spend the night for observation.

Given the suspicion of the agents assigned to protect her until they were certain the threat to Judge Pearson was over with, there was heavy distrust and dislike between them and the old biker.

Charlie finally had had enough. He leaned over Selma and gave her a quick kiss on her sleeping lips. "I'll be here to take you home when they'll let you out of here, babydoll." He knew she couldn't hear him, but it made him feel better for saying it. It was just as well that he went home and took a shower, he needed his arthritis meds, and some rest himself. He also needed to think about what he was going to do now.

All the way back to the duplex apartment where he lived, he thought about what he would be forced to do in order to live with Selma in his life. The only solution for him was to do what she'd asked him to do in the first place. *Fuck*.

He backed the Indian under the carport next to the 'Cuda. He bought the classic car as soon as he was released from the VA hospital in D.C. back in '70. It was kept in pristine condition, just like the Indian. It was his birthday present to himself before he'd shipped back out for another tour of duty. That tour had turned into a third, but he never regretted it. His country was worth the sacrifice. The handful of medals and even the purple hearts were just symbols now.

He came home for the last time in '74, a year before the last choppers left Vietnam, and the only reason he'd left then had been the explosion that rattled his brain, and sent one of his ribs through his lung. It had taken him almost a year to relearn the simplest of tasks. Thinking on his time in the rehabilitation center often made him feel guilty about the guys he hadn't been there to save. It had taken years, and thousands of miles, to come to terms that he couldn't save them all.

Seeing the way he and his fellow soldiers were being treated by an ungrateful nation took what little pride in his accomplishments during the war, and dropped them into a big pile of cowshit. He still helped his fellow veterans when he ran across one. The empty eyes and disillusioned look was almost universal with the homeless, and he always felt his throat tighten at the sight of yet another good man wasting away. Why had he been fortunate enough to be spared? The dumbest thing about all of it was that he'd put the uniform back on and take up arms again in a heartbeat if his country needed him. So would the thousands of homeless veterans across the country. It didn't matter their own country continued to betray them, even to this day, that oath of allegiance was burned into their souls.

He was sixty-two years old and felt every one of those years as he slid his body into the hot tub of water. The shower knocked the dirt off, but the tub would help ease his tortured muscles, and he laid back and let the heated water do its work. The water stung the nicks and cuts from the explosion, but the slice over his rib hurt like a motherfucker.

When he climbed out of the tub after the water cooled, he dabbed the slice and used butterfly strips to pull the edges of the wound together. He coated the entire thing with glue they called a liquid bandage, and hissed through the burn of the chemicals adhering to the wound. If he was careful the wound would heal fairly fast, and he'd have another scar for Selma to kiss better when she was finally back where she belonged, in his bed, and in his arms.

Grabbing a frozen dinner from his fridge, he nuked it and sat in his chair in front of the small flat screen to watch the news. Seeing the news that those cocksuckin' goat fuckers had beheaded another man pissed him off. "Why in the hell are we coddlin' these fuckers? Hunt every one of them sonsabitches down and drop 'em where they stand. Of all the dumb shit. Goddamned pansy-assed government we got."

He trashed the rest of the food and took a beer from the fridge to wash the pain meds down. His system was so used to his drink of choice that it didn't seem to have an affect on either the meds or the buzz he was looking for. The buzz didn't come to him, but he was so fuckin' tired that it wouldn't matter once he fell asleep.

He woke up feeling like shit and took a cold shower. Twice in the night he'd woken up from his nightmares, and the clammy sweat that had dried on his skin was washed away with the water down the drain. He toweled off and happened to see his naked form in the mirror. No matter which angle he saw of himself, nothing changed. He laughed at his own vanity, after all, "You was never a cover model for a romance book to begin with. What the fuck are you looking for? You let your ass fall apart, and now you want to see the muscles you used to have, you gotta' go back to work on them."

He wasn't flabby, his ass wasn't as tight as it'd been, and his balls hung a little lower, other than that he was the same as he'd always been to look at. A little older maybe, but not ready for the pine box yet either. He hated to shave his face, it had been years since he'd sported clean cheeks, but he gritted his teeth and set his jaw to the task.

Selma woke up feeling panicked. She looked around and remembered Charlie and how he came to her rescue.

A nurse came into the room and smiled at her. "Good morning, ma'am, I just need to take your vitals, and in a few minutes they will be bringing the breakfast trays up, so you can get some solid food onboard."

She waited until the nurse finished her task, and began asking questions. "What time will the doctor be making his rounds, and where's Charlie?"

The nurse pursed her lips and shook her head. "The doctor will be checking on his patients around ten this morning. I'm sorry I don't know anything about a Charlie. There's two officers stationed outside of the door, but other than them, I have no idea who you are talking about."

She didn't hear anything else the nurse said to her, didn't even acknowledge her leaving the room. Charlie wasn't here. She'd lost him again and, "Dammit to hell." She began throwing her blankets off her legs, and got so tangled up in the bedding that she was screaming in frustration by the time the nurse rushed back into the room with both officers on her heels.

The officers backed out of the room when they saw that no one was with the judge. She was red in the face and looked ticked off, they wanted nothing to do with a woman that pissed, regardless of what had caused it.

The nurse helped her exhausted patient untangle herself from the mess, and helped her to the bathroom before getting the woman settled back in the remade bed. "There now, I hope you are more comfortable, I should have asked if you needed to use the bathroom before I left, I am so sorry."

"Everything is fine now, thank you." She dismissed the woman. She wanted to wallow in her own misery, and didn't need some tender young nurse to see her while she did it.

Breakfast came and she drank the decaf coffee just for something to wet her throat, the eggs were ignored, but she ate the toast, and waved the aide who came to pick up the tray off. "Everything was fine, I'm not hungry." She felt like her stomach would revolt if she tried eating the gooey looking yellow clump of eggs, and her eyes kept stinging with the effort to hold back her tears.

The doctor came and after arguing with the man for fifteen minutes, he finally agreed she could be released. His recommendation that she, "Meet with a mental health advisor, I have a very good friend that specializes in PTSD, and other related traumas," was met with her angry glare.

"If I need to see someone I will, but I will choose my own if I choose to see someone. All I need is to go home and resume my life."

The nurse came in shortly after the doctor had left the room to help her dress in a set of clothing that she carried in with her. "I think I just met your friend and, girl, you are so lucky. I promised that I would have you ready and down to the main entrance in a half an hour. He said you might need these, and I can't believe there's another man on the planet that still opens doors for a woman. I don't know where you found him, but I want to get one like him for myself."

Selma recognized her clothing, and hearing that Charlie had come for her made her heartbreak from moments ago disappear. "My Charlie is a one of a kind, and my best advice for finding a good man is to find a bad boy, or in my case a bad man." She knew she sounded all smug and shit as Charlie would have said, but screw it. Her ol' man was here for her and she was *not* going to keep him waiting. She had to ask, "Did he bring the bike for the ride home, do you know?"

She had her head under the bright yellow pullover and didn't see the confused look on the nurse's face or she might have grown suspicious.

They were at the front doors of the hospital with the two officers behind her when she looked through the glass and saw the 'Cuda. Her grin turned to confusion when a man dressed in new blue jeans and a sport coat over a dark blue button front shirt walked through the doors. He smiled at her and she thought he looked familiar, even with the blackened eye and bruised cheekbone, but she tried to look around him for her man.

"Well, your Honor, are you ready to go home? The 'Cuda is warmed up and I thought we'd grab some take-out for lunch on the way to your place."

Charlie's voice coming from the stranger told her that her eyes were not in fact deceiving her. Gone was the long hair and his face was cleanly shaven. Her big bad biker man was gone, and in his place was Mr. GQ. She couldn't take her eyes off him as she was wheeled outside and he opened the car door for her and helped her to sit and, when he leaned down to click the lap belt in place, he stole a swift kiss before straightening up and closing her door.

He took the discharge papers from the nurse and thanked her before rounding the rear of the muscle car and getting into the driver's seat. He strapped the seatbelt over his slim hips, something she had never seen him do before. He drove them out of the hospital parking lot and he kept glancing at her, but she was having trouble forming words.

Finally she could say at least part of what was on her mind and watched his cheek turn red as she spoke. "I have never seen a more handsome man in my life." She slugged him in the shoulder. "Don't get a big head about that. I love the scruffy man more, he rides a big loud motorcycle and he, oh God, Charlie, why did you do this?" She knew why he'd done it.

He'd cut his long hair, shaved his whiskers and put his colors away for her. She wanted to yell at him, and to yell at herself for trying to change him in the first place. What had she done? "Tell me you didn't get rid of the bike." She was feeling guilty and choked on the words. "Tell me you still have the bike." He had always been neat and attractive in his appearance, but this stranger, he was just as sexy, just as considerate as her ol' man had been. But she wanted to cry for the loss of his beautiful long hair.

His gruff, "I still have the bike, I couldn't get rid of her just yet, we've spent a lot of years together, and I just couldn't part with her until I have to."

She slumped back into the seat in relief, at least that wasn't something she had to feel guilty about. "Thank You."

They stopped at the Chinese take-out place that they'd used many times before and he left the 'Cuda running, just in case she might get cold. She was too skinny for his piece of mind and he knew from the way his own clothing had started to bag on his body, that she must be feeling the same sadness that he had during their time apart.

He came back with a grocery bag filled with enough food to feed the entire club, but he figured they could eat leftovers for the next day or two if Selma didn't feel up to cooking, or she didn't have groceries in the house. Hell there'd been days he ate bologna sandwiches for breakfast, sweet and sour chicken would be a big step up from that. He was glad he had a cold case of beer in the trunk, he was sure that he would be needing it in the days to come.

They got to Selma's place and he came around to her side of the car to open her door and help her up from the low seat. When he picked her up and started walking to her front door, she found the voice that she seemed to have lost when they left the hospital. "What are you doing? You're going to hurt your back, I weigh more than I look you know."

He set her on her feet at her front door, reached into his pocket and pulled out the key to her house that he had kept after the break up. "You don't weigh nearly as much now as you did that day I had you pinned against your bedroom door. Do you remember that day, babydoll? I think about it all of the time. The way you rode me was something I can never forget or want to. It's no hardship to carry the woman I love. You must've forgotten that you can't wear shoes, those socks I brought aren't gonna keep your feet from getting hurt worse."

He gave her a little kiss on the nose, gently pushed her inside the door, and went back to the car to get their dinner and his beer. It was a nice neighborhood, but he locked the vehicle just in case some teenager wanted to try their hands at stealing the muscle car.

CHAPTER SIX

Selma had plates and chopsticks ready and forks for Charlie, who refused to never use "wooden toothpicks" to eat again once he left Southeast Asia. He uncapped a beer and handed it to her and she took the bottle immediately upending it to her lips, and he watched her slender throat work as she chugged back the cold brew. He waited until she placed the bottle on the table between her hands and looked up at him.

"I didn't do one fucking thing I didn't want to. You need a man that's respectable or one that looks respectable. This is as good as it gets. I bought a suit for the times we have to go out with your high-tonie colleagues, but this is my way of trying to fit in your life. We can go the fancy places you like so much and I'm aware that you are a lot younger than I am, so I don't want you to curb your fun thinkin' I won't be willing to go with you.

"I went to turn in my patch, but Big Dog told me to keep it." He looked away from her face, because the things Big Dog said to him weren't fit for her ears. Much of what the club Prez said pissed him off, but the rest, well the rest made his eyes sting. The fucker told him he would always be welcome, and as far as the Bastards were concerned, he was on vacation for an extended period of time.

He drank half of his own beer and sat down opposite his woman before deciding to get it all out into the open.

He reached out with his hand palm up, and waited for her to place hers over the top, when she did, his long fingers closed around her hand. "It's like this, when I cut you loose, it was the right thing to do. I wasn't ready to give up much for you until you weren't there. I'm a stubborn old fucker, and to pay me back for my selfishness, I didn't have you anymore. I about had a heart attack when those suits showed up and told me you had been snatched outta your home. I already felt like shit, but I went outside and finally listened to your messages." He choked a bit on the last few words as he recalled his feelings at the time.

"I let you down when you needed me, and I ain't gonna take that chance again. If I had been here with you, Birdsong would never have gotten his hands on you. I can't take back what's happened, but I can be here to make damn sure it don't happen again. If cutting my hair and becoming respectable is the price I have to pay for the privilege of being your man, to my way of thinking, it's a price I'm willing to pay."

He looked away from her, hell, he felt the fool for all this sharing of feelings, but she needed to know, and he might never get the gumption to have this conversation again. He'd always avoided getting involved, but he was as deep as he could get with this woman, and he gave up fighting the feelings he had for her.

"Without you, well my life wasn't so damn great, I was lost without you. It's gonna take some adjustment on my part, 'cause all I've ever been is a old scooter bum, I never locked down long enough to have a family, I got no kids, all I got is the 'Cuda and the scoot. If that's enough for you, then I'm your problem now, for as long as you want me."

Charlie watched as Selma listened to every word he said and when he finished speaking, she was out of her chair. She stumbled and ended up landing on his lap anyway, but it was exactly the spot she'd been headed for to begin with. Her hands cradled his smooth cheeks and her eyes locked with his.

"I love you, and I love that you are willing to try to be what I thought I needed you to be. If the time comes and you can't live this way any longer, promise me that you will tell me. Please promise that if you need to take a ride to blow off the pressure that you will jump on the bike and let the wind help. I want you to be happy to be here as much as you want me to be happy. Promise me, and then let's go celebrate in that big bed that's held too many memories for me to sleep in since you've been gone."

Charlie kissed her lips, and ran his hands over her slender body, "I'll be happy as long as we're together, babydoll, you took my greasy ol' heart and patched it up, it's yours now, girl, don't ever think I'll want the damn thing back.

Now you need to stand up and drop them pants if you want to keep 'em wearable."

His hands pulled the sweater up and over her head before she was completely on her feet. His shirt had too many buttons for him to deal with, so he pulled it up and over his head, dropped it on the floor, and began to loosen his belt. He never took his eyes from her body as she disrobed the rest of the way, right down to her skin.

"You are so beautiful, look at you, every time I see you like this it makes me need to take you as high as possible so you'll always want to be with me." His hands molded her breasts and allowed his thumbs to rake their rough texture across her nipples and loved the way her back straightened and thrust her breasts further into his work roughened hands. "It gives me a feeling inside when you show me that you need me as bad as I need you. Look at these little hard berries just waiting for me to suck on them." He bent his head and licked her nipple before opening his mouth and taking the nipple and areola inside. He didn't hesitate to suck strongly on the skin and whipped the sensitive nub with his tongue for long minutes while her hands tangled in his hair and held his head in place.

When he released that breast, his hand took over and his lips sought out its twin to treat to the same pleasures. His lips let her breast loose and traveled up to her neck to lick the spot under her ear. "Now, little girl, its time for me to have my dessert. I want you to lie down right here on the table, I'm gonna' grab a chair and make a meal of you. It's been too damned long since I had a taste of you, so don't expect much mercy, babydoll, I need this."

He had her clit in his mouth and was sucking on the small muscle hard. His tongue licked at the little muscle peeking from the hood of skin and his teeth scrapped over that while he sent a finger straight inside of her soaked pussy. Hearing her low scream only egged him on and he added a second finger to the first. Within seconds her hips tightened and she was clenching on his fingers and pushing her clit harder against his mouth and he let her ride that one out. If he hadn't jacked off twice this morning, he would have been inside her when that happened, and probably disgraced himself by coming with her.

He pulled his fingers out and began licking her from asshole to clit with long swipes of his tongue. He paused long enough to look at her, and couldn't help but feel the satisfaction deep in his chest for pleasuring her and putting that look on her face.

A man would kill to see that look on his woman's face. He bent his head and continued to keep her juices flowing for his efforts and her pleasure.

Selma grinned and sat on the tabletop. He was right, it had been too long since she'd enjoyed his brand of loving. The wood was cold on her back and she shivered, but she forget about the cold and hardwood under her when his hands spread her thighs and she felt his breath on her wet pussy. "Oh, Daddy, please, make me feel like you want me as much as I want you. I need this too, you know, and if I can walk when I get off this table, I plan to suck your cock until you haven't got a drop of cum left in your body. I want yo... Oh, Daddy."

She loved every swipe and stab of his tongue. She just came down from her second orgasm and her flesh was so sensitive that when his cock bumped her clit, she lifted her hips and gasped. No one, no one had ever made her feel so beautiful, and no one would ever take the place of the talented man now standing between her thighs.

"Give it to me, Daddy, let me feel you deep inside, I've missed you so much, and your cock will make up for a lot of lonely nights. Oh Yesss..." He took his time working his thick cock inside of her vagina, and she held her breath when his girth stretched the walls almost to the painful limits. This was her Charlie and he gave her everything she needed. "Oh Yes, I can feel every inch, yes, a little more, right there."

"Fuck, babydoll, I can barely get in, it's like the first time we did this, do you remember? So fuckin' tight." He pulled back and swiveled side to side to make a place for his cock in her velvety wet body.

As soon as he was seated, he bent down over her, and sweat dripped from holding back for so long. He settled into alternate short soft jabs, which morphed into the most powerful feeling of belonging that he'd ever felt any place. He wanted to laugh and yell at the same time, but not until he'd given her one more orgasm, she needed it and he damn sure needed her to keep needing him.

He leaned over her, smashing his cock as deeply as possible and began licking and nibbling at her breasts. He loved feeling her fingers tangled in his hair and pulling down so his attentions didn't stray from her breasts. He felt her pussy begin to throb and clench on his thickness, and blew out a breath of relief. He doubled the speed of his thrusts and she pushed up to meet his hips. He let go of his hold on the cum shooting from deep in his balls to fill her, as she yelled his name in her pleasure.

He picked her up from the table still impaled on his softening cock, and walked to the bedroom of the small house. He laid her on the bed and went to fetch a damp face towel to clean her up so she would be able to sleep in comfort. His woman was crying, and he knew it was from the release of the stress she'd been under, but it didn't set right with him to see tears fall from her beautiful eyes.

He wiped her face from the tears that continued to fall and she put up a small protest when he rolled her to her back to part her thighs to clean her pretty little pussy and inner thighs, taking the thick combination of their juices from each pass of the damp cloth. He took the cloth back to the bathroom and made sure he was cleaned before re-joining her in the bed. He took her into his arms and they fell asleep with him running his hand down her thigh where she'd gotten her first tattoo over a year ago. The butterfly was too girly to decorate his arms, but looked sexy as shit on the side of her ass. He was tickled to see that she'd continued to have the tat expanded on until it almost covered her entire thigh and hip. He fell asleep on the thought that he would explore the new additions to the picture with his lips tomorrow.

CHAPTER SEVEN

One month later…

Selma was again back in her courtroom presiding over the day's docket, and had just been handed a file to look at. She looked up toward the prosecuting attorney's table and saw him with his head close to the local sheriff's, and they were both staring at her as if daring her to say anything. Opening the file, she was surprised to see Pressley's name, and he was being charged with kidnapping and sexual assault. There was also a charge of resisting arrest and assault on a police officer. The officer in question happened to be the sheriff himself, and the victim just happened to carry the same last name as the sheriff's.

As she looked through the paperwork, she noticed there was no victim's statement, and no witnesses had come forward to substantiate the claims that Sheriff Houser had charged Pressley with. From the looks of him, it also appeared to her that Pressley should have had self-defense training because Houser did not appear to have a scratch on him.

"All right, Attorney Buel, I would like to know what we have here, I see a police report, sworn out by the father of the alleged victim, yet I see nothing more. How am I expected to rule on this without some sort of solid evidence."

The attorney stepped forward as if to approach the bench without her expressed permission until he caught the look she was giving him, and stopped in his tracks.

"Your Honor, may I approach the bench?" His words were spoken in a sneering manner and that pissed her off even more. She had to keep her composure, but it was hard for her not to charge him with contempt of court right on the spot. The man had been a pain in the ass since the day she took the bench as a judge, and he was still bitter by the defeat she'd handed him. His attitude was what had sank him in the voters' eyes, and she had just about had enough of his shit.

When he stopped mere inches from the bench, she leaned forward to tell him a few home truths. "I want to know what this arrest is based on, not just a pissed off father's concerns for his twenty-three-year-old wayward daughter, and I want to know why the prisoner is not in this courtroom while the charges are being levied against him. More importantly, I want to know what makes you believe you can come into this courtroom and speak in such a scathing tone to an elected judge. This is the last time you will speak to me in that manner or I will have you in front of a review panel."

He was turning red, and she knew he wanted to blast her with words, but he was not going to get the chance to do so.

"Now please answer the question, where is the prisoner, and why isn't he in the courtroom?"

"He is in the hospital, your Honor, there is a guard on him, but since he hasn't woken from the time the ambulance brought him in for care, we could not very well bring him in to face the charges."

She had to swallow the bile in her throat. Charlie loved that boy as if he was his own child, and he was not going to take this news easily.

"Okay, so the prisoner is in a coma, and where is the kidnap victim? I assume you at least have her stashed back at home in a safe place? Since there is no mention of her in this report, and the alleged suspect is in custody, I would like a detailed statement, one you know must be submitted to prove there was actually a crime committed. Do you have something for me to look at?"

He was shaking his head. "No, your Honor, the victim is still missing, Sheriff Houser has said in his statement the suspect came to the house to collect a ransom that he'd demanded and that is where he attempted to resist arrest and the assault on the sheriff occurred."

The idea that Pressley would do something like this was ridiculous, she had met him several times and unless she saw solid proof of his alleged wrong doing, she would not believe it. "So the ransom note must be available for the court to peruse."

He was shaking his head yet again. "Sheriff Houser swears the demand for ten thousand dollars was via his cell phone, and that his phone was trampled in the scuffle with the suspect."

He still wore that look that she hated while he stared at her. He was up to something no good and she knew exactly what that no good was. The sheriff was still standing by the prosecutor's table looking smug.

She waved Buel back to his place and spent time re-reading the documents sitting in front of her. Finally she made up her mind, it didn't set well with her to let this go, but she would leave that for an old friend of hers to decide.

"In light of the lack of prosecution's evidence, and the nature and familial status of the alleged victim and the alleged assault, I am sending this case to the State's Attorney General to decide whether or not to prosecute Elvis Collier. In the mean time, I also will recluse myself from this case to ensure justice is carried out in a manner that cannot be questioned due to my involvement on a personal level."

She smiled at Attorney Buel and Sheriff Houser. "Gentlemen, I suggest you get your facts in order and have your evidence ready to present to Dean Plyer, he does not suffer sloppy work, and you had better have a good reason for Mr. Collier to be in a coma, especially given the fact Sheriff Houser has no visible injuries or pain."

She smiled at the men who had attempted to lock her into a conflict of interest problem, and poor Pressley into prison without any chance to tell his side of the charges. They were whispering furiously to each other and she poked the bear one last time to make them aware she was on solid legal grounds here.

"I trust there is no objection to my decision, and I trust that Mr. Collier is receiving all necessary medical care to improve his health. Sheriff, I am certain you realize that without further proof, and the man dies, you will be facing manslaughter charges at the very least."

She rapped her gavel on the wooden square and the next matter was brought before the bench. Thankfully it was a straightforward breaking and entering case where the police had been waiting for the suspect to exit the pharmacy where they had broken into to steal drugs. Her concentration was shot to hell and back, and all she could seem to focus on was Charlie and what he would say about the charges leveled at his young friend.

Finally the last case came and went and she could go to her chambers and call him to find out what he knew about the subject. There was a voicemail from him that simply said, "I love you, babydoll, don't wait up, I'll be back in a week. I gotta do something for Pressley. Call Big Dog if you need anything. I'll be back, so keep the bed warm for me."

She texted his phone and knowing that he wouldn't look at it until he stopped for the night, or got to his destination, she said:

Will do, I love you too. Do what you can for him, I did all I could legally. Watch out for Sheriff Houser & Attorney Buel trouble brewing. Call me Daddy I miss you. Xoxoxoxoxo.

The x's and o's were an old fashioned way of sending kisses and hugs, but he would understand.

She went home and couldn't sit still for five minutes. She wanted to visit Pressley in the hospital, but knew her every move would be questioned and scrutinized. Knowing the young man was lying in the hospital without anyone who cared close to his bedside bothered her to no end, and she picked up the phone to call the club. Hopefully Big Dog would be there.

After vetting Tiny, the bartender and clubhouse caretaker, informed her that Big Dog was at school for parent/teacher conferences. Steven was in the second grade this year and Selma remembered the child well. He was actually the son of Big Dog's sister. When she died, the big man adopted the little boy as his own, and from all accounts the kid was flourishing under the care he received from his father and stepmother, Future.

Charlie had told her when they were eating dinner one night that Future was now pregnant and Big Dog was a nervous wreck. She smiled remembering the way he'd laughed about the tough guy being whipped and loving it.

He said something that stuck in her head and never left. "I was never fortunate enough to have kids of my own, I always wanted one or two little rugrats hanging around, but I never found a woman I'd want to be the mother of any kid of mine. Too bad we didn't meet twenty years ago." He'd leaned over and kissed her with longing and she'd wished they had met earlier too. He would be a wonderful father.

From all physical indications, she was going into menopause, but mother nature was dragging her feet on that. She never had children either, but that didn't mean she never wanted them. There had been a time when she actually had made an appointment with a fertility clinic to look into invitro with a donor's sperm. She'd chickened out at the last minute and canceled that appointment.

Maybe Future would allow her and Charlie to be honorary grandparents to the new baby. Not having a child was the one thing she regretted in her life, but a baby to love would help keep those regrets at bay. Even a borrowed one might help fill the void.

She shook her head at the brief fantasy that flashed through her mind. At forty–eight years old, she was too old to get pregnant and Charlie might have a few things to say about spending their retirement years raising a child. She wrote a note for herself to remember to ask Future if they knew the sex of the baby yet. Grandmothers were allowed to buy baby things, and she loved shopping for gifts. The thought made her smile and she opened her computer to see what there was in the line of baby needs nowadays.

By the time she looked at the clock it was already eight o'clock. So she stretched her arms above her head and moved the muscles around in a more comfortable position before reaching for her Rolodex and the landline that she kept for making private calls. She punched the numbers into the dial pad and waited for the line to be connected.

One of the perks of being a long term attorney and then a judge was having made contacts over the years, and she was taking advantage of her ability to call in favors now. The phone was answered on the fourth ring.

"This is Dean Plyer, what can I do for you, Selma?" The idea that he had her number startled her for a moment, but she remembered that they had gotten along well before, and the State's Attorney General would have Caller ID.

"Well hello to you too. I am calling about a case that came across my bench today, if you have time I'd like to discuss it with you?" She proceeded to tell him everything she knew and was gratified to hear his disgust at the shoddy way the sheriff and Buel had conducted themselves. "Also, you should know that I have recused myself from the case, the man I am with is good friends with the suspect, and it would be a conflict of interest if I tried to force the issue of the young man's treatment at the sheriff's hands. I know there is more to this than they are telling me, but again, if I get involved, the case will be a circus."

By the time she'd hung up the phone and hooked up her fax line, there was an order releasing Pressley from custody. Now all she had to do was talk to Big Dog and hopefully Charlie would call so she could give him the news.

He'd been so enraged when he saw Pressley lying in that hospital bed with his face a mangled mess, and the tubes sticking out of the kid's nose and mouth, that it was a good thing Show had been with him at the time to pull him back away from the room and the cop with a gun.

The Bastards knew what this was about, but no one thought for a minute that the sheriff would try to pull something so underhanded, or Pressley wouldn't have been sent to the fucker's place by himself. Now the kid was as close to dying as he could be without actually kicking heels up and dropping into a hole. Charlie was too pissed and concerned about the boy to wait to talk to Big Dog, and he and Show were on their way to Washington State. The proof exonerating Pressley was there, and if they didn't co-operate willingly, they damn sure would unwillingly. They should have dealt with that fucker, Houser, a couple of years ago when he came to them to find his runaway wife and daughter.

CHAPTER EIGHT

Houser had pulled Big Dog over to make his deal. The chicken shit fucker didn't have the balls to approach the Burning Bastards directly, no he had to make a production to cover his possibly being seen talking to one of the bikers.

He acted the part of the broken-hearted husband whose wife had taken his only child and ran away for some unknown reason. He agreed to the price, then had left the brotherhood alone for over the space of time it took the club to locate the runaways.

Once Demon and Knight had found the woman and teenager, and found out the reason for their leaving, the deal was off. They had spent weeks looking for the women and by the time the truth was brought out, Big Dog was not feeling charitable toward the sheriff, or the prosecuting attorney for that matter.

Marlene Houser and her daughter, Stephanie, were located in a travel trailer park outside of Corpus Christi in the gulf coast of Texas. The woman was working at cleaning and taking care of the elderly, and the daughter was waiting the counter at the local fast food restaurant. They had dyed their blond hair to dark brunette, and had some of the worst fake identification cards that either of the hunters had ever seen. It was obvious to the men that the two had been on the run for quite some time. The trailer they lived in was as simple as it got, and the few items of comfort that they could see were nothing compared to most females.

Demon insisted on making the interview a video call with Big Dog and Charlie was in the office at the time too, so he knew exactly what the deal was.

Marlene was embarrassed as she related the reasons for her leaving, "My husband, Sheriff Houser, is not an easy man to live with, he has appetites that no one sees but his family, and I put up with his abuse for years." She looked at Knight's kind eyes and continued her story after taking a drink of water, and reaching for her daughter's hand.

"Vince started bringing Howard Buel to our house, and into our bed." She saw Demon looking from her to her daughter and laughed bitterly. "I was a prisoner in my own home for the last six months we were there. My daughter didn't go to school. He told the school that we were teaching her at home. She patched me up when they were finished with me, often they left me bleeding and still tied up.

"The week before we left, the bastards had videoed themselves both having me at the same time, they left their faces out of the video, but told me if I left, they would plaster it over the internet with my face filled with a man's, well, you know." She had her daughter's hand cradled in both of her own when she looked back. "The morning after I saw Buel watching

Stephanie taking a shower. I knew we had to leave before he hurt her, it was just a matter of time and what he could offer Vince in return.

"I stole the neighbor's license plate and switched it out for mine, and waited until they left. I grabbed Stephanie and the video, and hit Vince's cash drawer. He has a drawer in the bedroom that has all kinds of valuables in it, well he did have one, he's probably moved it since we left. I took five thousand dollars and we headed east first, just in case he found someone that saw us leave town, and I drove a circle around to go west. The car is in Indiana at a rest stop, and we got a ride with a trucker to Texas. He could see that we were on the run. I guess the black eye and the fact than I was having a hard time moving told him everything he needed to know. He's the man that gave us the trailer, and I bought the truck for two thousand from a guy who was selling it on the way outside of Houston."

She let her tone change from embarrassed hesitancy to something close to fierceness. "We won't go back to him, I will kill him if I am forced to go back, I will kill both of them. No one touches my child. No one."

Big Dog had paid a visit to the sheriff and the man had of course denied the allegations at the time. The biker didn't turn a hair when he set the new rules for the sheriff, he would stop searching for his wife and daughter, and he would pay them a thousand a month to help with expenses, or the story would go to the press and both of the men could kiss their careers and asses good-bye. One of the Bastards would pick up the money each month and the club would make certain the women received the payments.

It had been almost a year since Vince Houser had paid his monthly stipend, and Pressley had been sent to deliver a message from Big Dog. Charlie wanted to be the one to deal with Houser, but Big Dog had shaken his head and reminded him that he was no longer an active member of the club, and gave him the choice of getting a signed affidavit from Mrs. Houser as to the nature of their disappearance and the timeline of their leaving. Or he could go home and wait for the brothers to deal with the problem. Show was assigned to keep him on course and out of trouble. It was a good thing they got along or trouble would have happened as soon as Charlie had heard what happened to Pressley.

The Indian ate up the miles to Washington State and he kept thinking about his lady and the rest of his life. He came to the same crossroads in his way of thinking, he was going to have to stop straddling the lives he was tippy-toeing between for the past month and a half. Either the club, or Selma, and the life they were building together. Choices fuckin' sucked.

Big Dog was asked to go to Selma's office, saying she had paperwork regarding Pressley, so when he arrived the next morning, he found her office and knocked on the door.

She gestured him into the room, asking him to have a seat. "Look, you are probably the tallest man I have ever seen in person, not including my college days. It hurts my neck to bend so far back to look at your face, and if I don't look at your face I am just about even with your waist." She smiled and watched as he sat hastily in the padded chair, but couldn't resist adding, "And we don't want me to have to stare at your zipper, now do we?"

Big Dog was still cautious around Selma Pearson. When they'd first met, she had been his nephew, Steven's, guardian ad litem. It was a fancy title for a child's attorney. She had fought against him being granted permission to keep custody and adopt Steven, all due to the fact he was the leader of the local MC club. The kid meant the world to him, since his mother who was Big Dog's sister, and her latest fuck buddy had died, Steven was his only living relative. Ms. Pearson had no idea how close she'd came to changing her mind.

If Charlie hadn't intervened, the woman would be lucky to still practice law in prison. The amount of drugs to put her away would have been expensive, but he would have planted them on her, and she would be spending ten to twenty locked up for something she was innocent of doing. Instead, with the sacrifices Charlie had made, she now sat on a bench doling out sentences to the 'criminal element' of the county. He still wasn't convinced that the woman was worth the price.

Seeing how miserable the greybeard had become since he rescued her from the shine maker, it didn't sit right. Knowing that he would have sacrificed just about anything for Future, his wife. He understood Charlie's thinking, but what kind of love was it going to be between the two older people. When only one is willing to give up everything in his life that made life worth living, while the other one kept her own lifestyle. A love like that would kill a man like his old mentor, and Big Dog considered her to be a selfish bitch.

He sent Charlie on a wild goose chase and he would swear he hadn't done any such thing before admitting he wanted to keep the old man out of trouble when the shit hit the fan. No one fucked with a brother, and the sheriff and his fuck buddy, Buel, were as good as dead. The wheels were in motion, and Pressley's father-figure would be nowhere around to draw suspicion. So now he would deal with the judge and go about his business.

"So what can I do for you, your Honor? We were enjoying a take-out pizza and a movie when you called. I'm sure you want to know that Steven is doing great in school and his teacher is happy with his progress."

"I recused myself from Pressley's case yesterday. In fact I decided to make sure the boy gets a fair shake. They have nothing other than the sheriff's statement. They wanted me to rule so they could accuse me of a conflict of interest and I am not as stupid as they believe me to be." Big Dog watched as she folded her hands on the desk in front of her and watched his face as she gave him the news.

"I sent the file to Dean Plyer, he is the Attorney General for the state, and I spoke to him last evening on the phone. We agreed that the sheriff is shady here, in fact Dean told me some rather interesting facts pertaining to the man. Long story short, I have an order from the attorney general releasing Pressley into your custody. You have sole responsibility to make decisions for him medically and in his personal dealings, and financial affairs. In short, you are now the temporary guardian of one Elvis Collier."

In no part of his imagination did he even consider that she would have gone to such lengths to help one of the Bastards. He studied the papers in front of him and saw the signature. Being a member of an MC group was always a gamble when it came to the law. He didn't trust any public servant that carried a badge and a gun. Logic told him that the majority of cops were decent people just doing their jobs. The faction of abusive fucks tarnished all of them in the eyes of most biker communities. Houser was one of the bad ones and should have been double tapped a few years ago.

He nodded his head and began to stand, but her next question tested his code about staying out of the brother's personal business.

She'd done them a solid and he was not going to lie to her in return.

"I want to know if Charlie is still a member of the Burning Bastards, or did you kick him out when he came to stay with me, it's a simple question, and I want an answer if you please. He smiles at home, and I know he still rides his bike, but I know he isn't happy. He acts like his best friend died even when he tries to smile for my benefit. I'm not ashamed to say I love him, don't you understand? I want him to be happy."

He stood and went to the door, turned back and asked her, "Well, the way I see it. He has given up everything he is to be with you. I'm not talking about the hair and beard here, he hides his tats, he doesn't wear his colors, and the few times he does ride, he rides away from here most of the time, so people that know you don't get offended. Let me ask you a question. How much more of his life will you demand he give up for you? You already have his balls in your purse, what's next, you want him to open a vein so you can sit in a courtroom and lord it over anyone unlucky enough to be dragged in front of you? He'll do it, because that's the kind of man he is.

"Now is where I say thank you for helping with Pressley, I'm going to the hospital and kick the first motherfucker who refuses to let me see him in the goddamned head."

Selma knew the man didn't like her, in fact she understood his dislike very plainly, but this had nothing to do with her call, that's why she had laid it all out for the man rather than a snippet here and there.

But when Big Dog finished with his take on Charlie, Selma shut her opened mouth. She knew the big man wasn't happy about Charlie's decision to change his lifestyle and looks. It was way beyond anything she'd previously considered. It appeared that she had some serious decisions to make too. From the way Charlie had spoken and acted about the change, she knew he was doing his best to adjust, and she thought he was beginning to enjoy talking to people who weren't affiliated with the club. He even watched a few chick flicks with her and let her cry on his shoulder during the sad parts.

Hearing Big Dog's take on the situation put the relationship in an entire different light. What kind of woman who loved her man was she? She'd taken all that he had given her and what had she given him in return besides her time and love. "Face it, woman, you didn't want to see what you've done," she said as she sat waiting for the answers to come to her until the clerk came to inform her that the first cases were entering the courtroom.

She nearly groaned aloud when she read the first case file. Billy Moon, also known as Mooney, was accused of trespassing for the second time at the local pancake house, he refused to leave when they asked him for the third time to stop going into the ladies bathroom. He had small mirrors glued to the tops of his shoes, and would hide in the stalls until an unsuspecting woman would need to relieve herself. His foot would slide under the stall partitions and hoped to gain a peek-a-boo shot at the lady. The last woman had taken umbrage at his perving and waited until he came out. She had beaten him with her purse and stomped on his toes, breaking the mirrors.

"It's going to be a long day," she said out loud to herself as she walked into the courtroom.

CHAPTER NINE

Sheriff Houser got home and busted a new hole in the first wall inside his door. Howard Buel shouldered his way past the seething man and went straight for the cabinet he knew contained the alcoholic beverages, grabbed a tumbler from the cupboard next to it, and walked to the fridge to get some ice for his drink.

Vince was cussing a blue streak and he waited until his friend ran out of words before handing the glass over to the irate man. The empty glass was shoved back at him, and he looked at the barely melted ice cubes before turning back to replenish his drink.

"That interfering bitch, why couldn't she play along, what the hell? We had her cold on this one, if she'd just dismissed the charges, we would have had her and whether she wanted to co-operate later wouldn't matter. You said she was in love with one of those fuckin' Bastards. He would strangle her if she let one of the brothers get railroaded. What's wrong with the stupid whore?"

Howard was just as pissed as Vince was, but he'd learned long ago to redirect that rage into planning. He mind was imagining ways and means to get them out of the heavy scrutiny of the state people that had been kind enough to notify them that the investigators would be in town before ten in the morning.

Judge Selma Pearson would pay. She'd beaten him in the election by over two hundred votes, and that still stuck in his throat. Vince was right, she was a fucking whore.

"Look, we can weather this, all we need is a better story about the kid and the disappearance of Marlene and Stephanie. The police in Elkhart still have no leads or witnesses around where she stashed the car. The place is rural and no one would notice the car for days if not weeks. So if we can't find them, they can't find them either, there should be no problem sticking with the plan right? They are gone and you suspected the biker gang kidnapped them right? So the kid came by to collect the ransom money and you refused, he jumped on you and you put his head into the wall. You have been distraught and needed to amend the complaint."

He put his hand on the sheriff's shoulder, drank a few swallows of the drink, and handed it over to the trembling mad man. "Here you go, buddy, if we stick to the same story, we'll be fine." He grinned and said, "Just think, we get to plan a nice thank you for the judge. When everything is said and done, and the state boys go home, we can give Selma Pearson and her biker fuck boyfriend something to think about before we kill them."

The sound of clapping startled the men and they turned to see Big Dog leaning against the doorjamb clapping his hands and smiling. Vince reached for his side arm and heard the sound of a shotgun being jacked back and forth in a rapid sound. He held his arms away from his body, and felt the Glock taken from the holster at his side. "What do you want?"

The laughter rumbling from the huge motherfucker grated on his nerves. He glanced over his shoulder and changed his mind about attempting a run for it. The Bastard the club called Blue had a twelve gauge sawed off locked and loaded on him, and the fucker was grinning.

Howard opened his mouth to say something but thought better of it until he finished the last swallow of his drink, and hurtled the glass at the doorway where Big Dog had just moved away from. "Fucker." The fist to his face was a surprise, and it made him see stars for a second before he swung his balled up hand toward the big fucker. His fist connected with the biker's wrist, and without understanding how it happened, his wrist was grabbed and his arms were pulled behind his back while Vince's handcuffs went around his wrists. "Look, we can make a deal, your club will be off limits in this county, as long as you don't fuck around and get sloppy so there are no witnesses, you all can run the place, right, Vince?" He looked at the Sheriff, who was now holding his pistol with the help of another hand encased in a black leather glove holding his finger on the trigger.

"What the hell? Vince, don't let him make you do it, we're friends for God's sake, no one will believe you killed your best friend in cold blood." The sound of the .40 caliber round being shot was the last sound he heard with any clarity. He looked down to his chest and saw the bright red pattern of his life's blood rushing to the bullet hole and escaping onto the former white shirt.

The gun was removed from the sheriff's fingers and he knew he would be next. Nothing he could say would change the biker's mind.

"You know, I tried to deal with you in an honorable fashion, and look at the way you treat me and my brothers. You are the arrogant fuck here, asshole, first trying to get us to bring you an abused slave and a teenager who was being groomed to be that fucker's toy. Then you fucked with a kid, one of us. You already know you're going to die tonight, but I plan to make you beg for it before I let you kill yourself. I'll even give you some hope that you can walk into the sunshine in the morning. All you have to do is win the fight, all you have to do is knock me out before I make you wish you're mother had spit you out when your goatfuckin' daddy screwed her. See? I fight like a man. So take your best shot, motherfucker."

Within mere seconds after he made contact with his fist to Big Dog's chest, he was tossed around like a basketball hitting the wall. He kept getting up, it was his only chance to live, but when he landed face first in Howard's chest, with his mouth lying in Howard's blood, it was too much. "Just get it over with, shoot me and let's end this now."

Big Dog hauled him upright and shook his head at the big talking corrupt son-of-a-bitch. "I told you, you need to beg, I don't do well with demands, and you seem to think I'll pull the trigger. What about the words 'you are going to shoot yourself' didn't you understand?"

He was held upright while the huge hands slapped his face a dozen times, the last time it happened it felt like his neck snapped. "Alright, alright, give me the fucking gun." He looked toward Big Dog, "Please." His words were slurred and hard to understand from the split lips and the inside of his mouth being shredded by his own teeth.

The same hand as before helped him hold the pistol to the side of his neck with it angled slightly up. He expected that black-clad finger to press on his own trigger finger, but the guy said, "You want to die, pull the trigger, I ain't your executioner, you will be." He took a deep breath and said a silent prayer that God would forgive him before pressing the warm metal beneath his finger. The shot exploded and he felt as if his head bad blown apart, but he could still see the men staring at him. He tried to say something, and closed his eyes for the last time.

Blue spoke up. "The only problem I see here is the sheriff has been beaten bad, and the fucker on the floor hasn't got a scratch on him."

Big Dog shrugged, "Not our problem if they were smoking and caught the whiskey on fire, now is it? Come on, drop a few bottles around and I'll light a cigar."

"Not trying to tell you what to do, but the canyon drop off is right down the road a half a mile. Why waste good booze and a nice place like this when the canyon and a gas can is so close by?"

Big Dog looked at the younger man with new respect, "I guess you're right, Blue, why waste anything more than a car and the energy."

Show checked his phone for the fifth time and Charlie wondered what that was about. They were camped out near a forest just over the Oregon state line for the night, and should be in Washington the next day early in the afternoon. From then they should find a little burg called Graham, and that is where the two women were supposed to be hiding out.

It didn't take Show long to tell him what was going on, and Charlie was furious when Show said, "I half expected this, Big D says abort and come home, the situation is handled. I guess we made the trip for nothing." He watched the old guy begin to toss rocks and small limbs toward a pine twenty feet away. "You know something, brother, I don't care, I needed the ride to blow the stink off anyway. It's been a good trip with good company, a man can't ask for more, can he?"

Charlie was pissed, he knew in his gut he'd been sent off to get him out of the way, and when he saw Big D he was going to tell him his thoughts on being coddled like an infant. The thing was, Show had a good outlook on the trip and he knew he needed the freedom of not worrying what people would say to Selma, or think about her hanging with an old scooter bum like him. He needed this more than he would admit to anyone.

This love shit was complicated, and he wondered if he would break out of the new arrangements in his life. He kept the certainty in the back of his mind that one day he'd wake up and she would tell him to leave. The shoe was on the other foot with Selma, it had been from the beginning. Before, he'd always been the one to say it wasn't working out for him and the woman he was with at the time. Now he was waiting for his walking papers and it was wearing on his soul.

CHAPTER TEN

It took Charlie and Show two days to get back home and Charlie went directly to the clubhouse before he went home. It wasn't that he didn't want to see Selma first, but he had unfinished business with a certain smart fucker and it was best to take care of it now and get it over with. Show left for his place in town, and Charlie waved him off at the turnoff to town. He went another mile and swung the bike into the open gates at the club.

When he walked into the place, there was almost no one around. Tiny wasn't behind the bar and even Joker wasn't at his customary spot by the door. Candy was wiping down tables and she smiled when she saw who had entered this early in the morning. He nodded his head at her but kept walking to the back of the building where Big Dog's office sat. He didn't bother to knock, and was disappointed when he found the room as empty as the main room. He went back to the bar and asked Candy where everyone was at?

She was still smiling at him, but shook her head, "As far as I know, Big D took Future to some specialist out of town, I heard they'd be back in a day or two. Demon and Knight left around four this morning, and Tiny is at the dentist to get his new dentures, another tooth fell out last week and he got tired of trying to eat through a straw. You can tell he's lost some weight 'cause his pants are starting to bag on his big ass."

He thanked her and left the building. Fuck, he hated it when he had a full head of steam and didn't have a place to vent. It was Wednesday and Selma would still be at the courthouse working, so he mounted up and rode to his old place. He wasn't sure of the reason he'd kept the place after moving most of his shit in her place. Not that there was much more than his clothing and a few pictures to move in the first place. Most of his old clothes were still here. His new duds were hanging in her closet.

He gathered some clothes onto the bed, and headed for the shower, maybe he needed to have some solitude today. He came to a few decisions on the trip home, and he wanted to think it through one more time before he acted on instinct again.

He was dead tired, but his mind refused to shut the fuck up, so he wrapped the towel around his waist and walked into the kitchen to grab a beer, before sitting in his favorite chair and flipping through the channels. The noon news was on and he sat up straight when the breaking news reporter came on the screen with a fire and rescue truck behind her as she told the audience that "The police were not releasing the names of the victims of something they are saying appears to be a murder-suicide. Neighbors say the victims of the wreck are Sheriff Vince Houser and

Prosecuting Attorney Howard Buel. That has not been confirmed pending forensic evidence and a coroner's report."

"Well the fuckers took care of it alright, but what happens to Pressley now?" He would wait to talk to Big Dog, but Selma would be home in five or six hours, so he had time for another brew and watching the remainder of the newscast.

He woke up and some crime show was on and it was full dark outside. "Shit, it's almost fucking cold in here." He remembered shutting the heat down to a temperature that wouldn't allow the pipes to freeze if they got cold weather while he wasn't there. He looked at the clock and it was after nine and decided to wait until early in the morning to go home. He hadn't counted on falling asleep like that, and she would be ready for bed by now. He was wide awake and she would try to stay up to keep him company. That was just the kind of woman she was. She always put him first in everything but the one area where it counted.

There was a frozen dinner and a frosted over hamburger that had been tossed in the freezer before he'd left the last time, so he nuked the dinner, wishing it was a plate of Selma's chicken and potatoes instead of the mushy shit that he used to enjoy eating.

She knew he was back, on the way home from work she'd stopped for gas and ran into Show while he was filling the tank of his bike. He had been at the clubhouse, that was as much as she did know for certain. Maybe he had too much to drink and stayed overnight. Pictures of some of the housecats and passarounds flickered through her mind, but she knew that her man wouldn't do that to her, tempted by perky tits and firm thighs or not. No, Charlie wouldn't stray.

She stretched out on the sofa and used the remote in front of the television to watch the ten o'clock news cast. She had already been informed of the deaths of the sheriff and Howard Buel. It appeared that the sheriff had Howard in handcuffs before the attorney's sedan had gone over the side of the deep canyon. She was glad Charlie had been out of town when it happened, because she might have wondered if he had help engineer the accident. She had no doubt the two men were "taken out" by the MC, no one messed with a brother and walked away scot-free. Not that Charlie had ever said anything. When she began dating the charismatic biker, she'd gone online and read up on as many sites as she had time to see if bikers actually were as bad as they were reputed to be. She found more information than she knew how to process at the time.

The 1%ers were what she might refer to as lawless, yet they had their own laws and codes to live by. There were varying degrees of toleration anywhere from drugs to slavery and prostitution, grand theft, and payments made to the clubs to allow people to do business as long as they paid each month.

Then there was the borderline clubs. She imagined that the Burning Bastards were such. They worked security for rock stars, worked their version of bounty hunters, and most of them had jobs or businesses. From there it trickled down to church groups and wanna be's. All biker groups seemed to have a heart regardless of the percent they lived as. They organized and ran toy drives for underprivileged children, they arranged and rode in cancer fund raising. They took some of the more spry and alert patients in nursing homes for rides to let them feel the wind one last time. Or for the first time. It seemed poker runs were a favorite fundraiser for bikers and they had raised millions for the causes over the years. All in all, they were just regular people attempting to raise their families and make a decent living for themselves. She could respect that.

She had tomorrow off, and she would track him down if she had to. Thumbing off the TV, she laid back in the familiar cushions, pulled the knitted afghan from the back, and covered her body to keep the chill off.

She was awakened by a kiss on her shoulder, and she smiled. He was back, and her world was right again. She was lying face down on the sofa with her head hanging over the side, and when she looked back to say good morning, she felt her shorts being peeled down her legs and pulled off one foot, and left to dangle off of her ankle.

His fingers were busy between the folds of her greedy pussy and she felt the wetness slide from her vaginal tunnel lubricate his fingers as they set a rhythm that made her need to move her hips. "Oh, Daddy, I missed you, this feels so good."

His fingers withdrew and she was humping onto air then made out a small scream of frustration that turned into a hum when his thick cock penetrated her pussy. With her legs spread as far apart as possible in this position, his cock slid in easier than normal, or maybe it was the juice from her cunt that made the glide less difficult. Whatever it was she grunted when he hit bottom and she felt his cocks head kiss her cervix. His hand reached down and cradled her throat in a light but firm hold, slowly applying pressure with each stab of his cock. He knew this drove her crazy, and when he began talking dirty to her, she stopped trying to hold back. When he was like this, she was in for the fucking of her life and each time was better than the last.

"You like that, dontcha, you make me want to fuck your sweet little pussy for hours, and maybe I will. Should I keep you naked and sucking my cock and fucking all day? I bet you love the idea of me slapping this pretty little ass, don't cha? Come on, babydoll, it's time for you to let me feel your pussy grab my cock and suck the cum from my balls. Yeah, darling I love it when you wake up as wet as any slut trolling for a random fuck." He rammed her harder and gave her thigh a swat of his big hand and she screamed as her hips slammed back onto his cock. "Come on, doll, yeah, I feel your tight cunt clenching and pulling me deeper, fuck yeah." He flooded her pussy with his cum even as she gasped and he felt her do something only a few women he'd been with before could do, she clamped down on his cock so hard that he couldn't move until her body relaxed enough to unclench her pussy from its stranglehold on his shaft.

"Goddamn, woman, you should have a tat on your ass that says "caution", fuck me if you shouldn't". I'm glad your pussy let me go so we can get something to eat and I will pet her afterwards, I feel like staying in today, I hope you don't have any plans besides making your man happy."

She smiled and rolled over to see him standing next to the sofa with his clothes in his hands. He might be in his early sixties but the man was still built like a man should be. Small hips and waist up into wide shoulders and, damn, she could feel herself becoming interested again and had to look away from his muscled chest. She sat up and fell backwards onto the cushions, dizzy from the rapid movement. She held out her hand for him to pull her upright and she found herself in his arms with his clothing smashed between them as he joined her in a good morning kiss.

Over breakfast and into the early afternoon she related everything that had gone on with the sheriff and when the subject of Pressley came up, he turned the subject to her fast thinking. "I'm damn glad that you got Big Dog to be his guardian. He will make sure the boy gets all the help he needs from here on out."

She wanted to tell him that she had made a decision, but he kept changing the subject for the entire day and into the evening. He didn't want to talk about the two of them and it worried her. The last time he'd made love to her was too sweet and gentle for mere words, and she felt tears sliding down her cheeks. She knew what he was doing, and it broke her heart all over again.

"You're leaving again, aren't you? Will you be back or should I try to move on again? Tell me what I've done this time to make you want to leave me, to leave us. I begged you the last time, and it did no good, all it did was make me feel like a fool for begging you to love me enough to stay. Is that what you want from me again, to see me on my knees? I'll do it, tell me what you need from me to make you stay, don't do this please."

Charlie rolled over and raised his hand to cradle her face. "Babydoll, I love you, ain't nothing gonna change that. I need to get my head on straight. It's not about what you can do or what I want from you. Hell, woman, I know I'm a stupid fucker for even thinking I need to do some soul searching, but every breath I take tells me I need to go for a while, I'll be back when I get my shit together, I hope you're still waiting for me, but I won't expect you to wait around for me. I want to beg you to promise me that you understand, but even I don't understand it myself, how can I expect you to?"

He rolled onto his back and pulled her over until her head rested on his chest. "I never met a woman who could hold me, never met one who I handed my heart to with both hands like I did you. I will be back, and if you still want me, we'll make this life a permanent thing. I'll be ready to give up the club, and do my damndest to settle into your life. It's all I can promise, and I hope it's enough for you. Now go to sleep and I'll lay here knowing I am an old fool."

She eventually fell asleep still making little whimpering sounds, but he took his pillow and slid it between her arms as he slipped out of the bed.

CHAPTER ELEVEN

She knew he was gone before she opened her eyes. She felt like shit and once she looked in the bathroom mirror, she knew she looked as good as she felt. A hot shower improved the looks a little bit and the light coating of make-up disguised the blotchy red spots on her skin from her crying jag.

Heading into the kitchen seemed like a waste of energy, but she desperately needed coffee, and there was only one way to get it this morning. There was a very small jewelry box sitting on the kitchen table, and she reached a trembling hand to pick it up and opened it to reveal a beautifully set diamond ring. The ring was white gold and was the most beautiful thing she'd ever seen. Her eyes were swimming again and she picked up the single sheet of paper and tried to read it through her tears.

Babydoll, I know I'm no great catch, but I love you. I have the band that goes with this ring, and when I get back I hope you will consent to wear both of them. I don't know fancy words, but whether you wear it or not, I'll always be yours.
Charlie

Coffee was forgotten. She sat on the nearest chair and held the box for a long time.

Eventually she took the ring from the box and slipped it on her finger. He was rough, and he was an ass, but she was going to be the best wife he would ever ask for. The ring didn't make up for his absence, but it went a long way to restoring her faith in him. He would return to her.

It took her extra time to repair her make-up and find her shoes, but she made it to the courthouse in time to peruse the files for today. There was a junior attorney for the prosecution, but nothing that appeared to be too complicated was scheduled for today. She made a pot of coffee in her chambers and sat back to enjoy her first cup of the day. The ring flashed and she held up her hand to admire the beauty of the setting against her hand.

The cases were mostly slam dunk against the accused. One man had stabbed his girlfriend multiple times because she had taken the power cord for his game box and refused to return it until he got a job. He had no remorse and she had to have him removed from the courtroom because he would not shut up.

Another case involved a mother of three who refused to give up an abusive boyfriend and the man had begun hurting the children. The children's natural father stared at the woman with hatred in his eyes and the boyfriend must have either been high or drunk. She had the bailiff remove the boyfriend and lock him up for public intoxication and contempt of court. Charges of child endangerment were serious, but the woman sat with her lawyer through the proceedings until Selma wanted to slap the smile from her face every time the ex-husband accused her of more misdeeds. Needless to say, the father won custody of the children and the mother was ordered to undergo psychological testing to determine if she had a mental problem, or should be tried for her crimes against her children. The natural father received sole custody pending the resolution of the mother's case.

The last case on her docket made her frown as she read it. A young tough named Sam Lorne was accused of felony firearms possession. The further down she read the report, the more pissed off she became. It was a damned BB gun with no BBs and the kid was in the woods when the good sheriff arrested him for the firearm charge and for destruction of private property and vandalism.

The boy was small framed and almost feminine in appearance. She had heard rumors about the sheriff before and now she was certain she knew what had happened. The kid's parents were sitting behind him, and the mother was dabbing at her eyes. The kid was staring at her defiantly and she noticed the homemade tats on his bony arms. He was slumped in his chair and sneered at his court appointed attorney.

The D.A.'s attorney stated the dry facts of the case and sat her happy little ass back down. The suspect's attorney wasn't any help to his client. More than likely the kid never saw him before an hour ago. This kind of thing made the court system look bad, and she almost hated her job at the moment. When she lifted her fingers to both attorneys indicating them to follow her into her chambers, the kid looked nervous. Good, let him stew for a while, she had things to talk to the lawyers about.

She took her time addressing the two people in front of her. What she said caused the lawyer from the D.A.'s office to set her jaw and narrow her eyes.

"What in the hell do you call this, Ms. Sullivan? No witness statements, no addresses of the alleged vandalism, nothing, you bring me a big nothing with the signature of a dead man who cannot be questioned now. I certainly hope that this is not an indication of your performance as a prosecutor. If you went to law school and learned anything, you might have learned the term 'Lack of Evidence'."

She turned her ire on the defense attorney next. "Give me one reason that I shouldn't advise your client to sue you for failure to perform. I've had less than ten minutes to look over the file, and you've had how many weeks to punch holes in the cartoon case?

"I am going back into that courtroom and I am going to propose the young man enters into a mentor project that I am organizing. Do not misunderstand me, I refuse to sentence him on the current charges, those will be dismissed, and I will entertain the idea of him being a public menace.

"If the two of you ever decide to bring something like this to my courtroom again, I will make you very sorry. You bring evidence, or do not let me see you again. You," she pointed her finger at the chastised defense attorney, "I defended innocent people as a younger attorney. I never went into the court without speaking to my client at least twice. I also never allowed a client to be railroaded like you have done with this young man."

Now that she'd thought of the perfect way to deal with some of the juvenile and very young adult offenders, she figured that she had better hold up her end. She had to find mentors and apprenticeships for the young people to report to, or they would be back on the streets and getting into even more serious trouble with the police.

After court was over, she headed to the Bastard's clubhouse. Several of the members owned and operated businesses and she hoped to get some volunteers for her pilot program. Hopefully there would be a few of them there this evening.

Tiny smiled at her when she walked in, but most of the men sitting around or playing pool glanced her way to see who had come in, and then ignored her. She knew that they didn't trust her, but she wasn't about to let that deter her. This was important and it would go a long way to bridging community relations.

"Hi, Tiny, I hoped to catch Big Dog if he has time to speak to me?"

Tiny handed her a longneck and nodded to the man at the end of the bar. "Sure thing, Selma, Blue will see if Big D has time to chat with the judge wontcha Blue?" The biker walked toward the back of the building where the office was.

"So what's new? Have you heard from that old fucker lately? He came in here a day or two ago and had words with Demon and Knight, and he didn't stop by me to talk. All he did was wave like a beauty queen when he walked by me."

She laughed at the description of Charlie in a focused mood. "I haven't seen or heard a word from him, but he's only been gone for a couple of days. He promised to keep in touch, so I expect I'll hear from him tomorrow sometime."

Blue came back and waved at her to follow him to where Big D was. She waved at Tiny with the beauty queen gesture and made the big man laugh as she passed the length of the bar.

She noticed the hostility right away and wondered what happened to renew his case of mad at her. She had antagonized him at one time, and the man appeared to not be the forgiving type. As Charlie would say, fuck it, all he can do is say no. She decided to go for broke.

"Thank you for taking the time to talk to me, I have several things to discuss, but I want you to know that I received the paperwork for the dismissal of charges on Pressley, the charges are dropped and since the sheriff is no longer with us, there was no reason to continue with the charade." Big Dog nodded but sat back in his seat with his hands folded across his ribs.

"Second, I have decided to try to get a mentoring program up and running for some of the "at risk" young people in the community. I know that several of the club's members are business owners and might be persuaded to take on a kid that needs more help than their parents can provide. Would you ask the membership if they would be so kind as to take on a volunteer spot to teach these kids how to keep themselves out of trouble?"

The big man began to laugh, and once he pulled himself together, he looked right at her with disgust. "Lady, you and those like you always try to find a way to fuck with lowlifes like us. Suppose we took these dregs of society kids on and they still fuck up. We both know that the club and brothers would catch the shit from that too. You'd say we were teaching the little saints to turn to a life of crime, but then, what can you expect from biker scum." He shook his head and sat up straight in his chair.

"My answer to you is fuck you and whoever else is backing your scheme. Get some of your high class fucks to give the little pukes a job. You've made it obvious in your feelings about the Bastards, and there isn't a man here who would help you cross the road if it weren't for the love and respect we all have for Charlie."

She had heard enough. "How dare you talk to me that way. You don't know me, your prejudice against the law is choking you and blinding you to the fact that laws are needed and people are needed to enforce those laws. My plan is to get some of these kids into apprenticeships to keep them off the street and give them a direction. Most of the men I've met here appear to be good men with stable work and thriving businesses.

"I am sick of seeing these kids turning to crime to keep them busy and occupied while parents are too busy or too downtrodden to care what their kids are up to. I had a young tough guy in my courtroom today that had nothing but contempt for his parents, his lawyer, and the court too. He has some impressive tattoos that you could tell he'd done himself. Do you know the first thing that popped into my mind? I thought about Freakshow and the beautiful tats that I have seen him do. That is what gave me the idea for mentors.

"By the way, what makes you think I consider you lowlifes? For God's sake, Charlie is one of you and I sleep with him. I have never said a word against your organization since Charlie brought me into the fold and I am baffled by your accusations."

"Lady, I think it's time you left. You haven't earned the right to speak or speculate about this club or its members. We all know the only reason you stepped in for Pressley was to keep Charlie from going ape shit on your fuckwad sheriff.

"Although it would be interesting to see you sitting on your throne judging him in court now, wouldn't it. That's something you will have to think about too. Cops love nothing better than to harass bikers, they will lie, trump up charges, and do their damndest to pin any crime on a biker. What's gonna' happen when one of us goes to jail and then we are brought in front of you? Charlie turned in his colors to keep you from having to worry about whether you would sentence one of us to prison or worse."

He pointed his finger at her and his voice steadily rose until the last words were nothing less than a shout. "You're the reason he quit, and for that, lady, I hope you rot in hell for taking his family and his freedom. Now, you selfish bitch, get out of here before I toss you out on your skinny ass."

Selma was stunned, she'd never asked Charlie to give up the close knit family unit that he had with the Bastards. She never wanted him to have to choose between her and the group of men that were closer than brothers. She tossed her hands in the air, and let them flop into her lap. Standing up, she continued to face the man that Charlie spoke of with such affection.

"I never asked him to leave the Bastards, I never wanted to put him in the position that you are describing, and I never look down on people. For your information, and not that I consider it any of your business, but I was raised in juvie and foster homes. My parents were the lowlife dregs you are harping about and the last time I saw them, they were headed to prison and I was headed to juvenile detention. I act like a lady by choice, not because I want to lord it over other people. And Mr. Smartassed-Fucker, I do make a difference in people's lives. So I'm not versed in biker regulations, I am human. You cut me I bleed, you piss me off and I get mad, you fuck with my man and I'll be the one doing the cutting. Ignore his resignation, he will be back."

She turned to walk to the door, but turned with her hand on the doorknob. "All you had to do was to pick up the phone and talk to me. We could have avoided this conversation and gotten everything taken care of in a friendly manner. I might be going to hell, but when you die, just remember, I'll volunteer to drive the bus to pick you up and I guarantee it will be an interesting trip."

She turned the knob and walked out of the door, quietly shutting it behind her. She looked up and saw the hallway was packed and had to shake her head. She shrugged her shoulders and tried to smile. "He's still breathing, his face is red, and steam is blowing out of his ears, but he's alive."

The crowd backed out of the small area and she walked out of the building with her head held high. She'd be damned if she would let any of them see her break down and cry.

CHAPTER TWELVE

Charlie was headed home. He'd gone to the Vietnam Memorial in Washington D.C. and read every name on the wall. A bare handful were familiar to him, and he took the time to remember and at times speak to the person who had given his life for his country. By the time he walked out of the memorial, he finally felt the heaviness in his heart lighten. His name should have been on that wall. By the grace of God and the survival skills he used at the time, he'd been spared.

He hadn't been the only veteran that held a one-sided conversation with the dead, and somehow it helped him understand that feeling of guilt for being alive when more deserving men had died. He talked with a few of the old guys, and wiped unashamed tears from his own face, seeing that some were in wheelchairs, some with missing limbs, and even one young man in an Army uniform was there to visit with his grandfather's shadow. The kid was headed for Afghanistan the next day and Charlie sent up a prayer for God to carry this boy through until it was time for him to come home, and make a family that his grandfather could watch over and be proud to see his legacy carry on.

His stomach had been bothering him for a week before he stopped in at a clinic in Pennsylvania, and they gave him some chalky shit to coat his stomach, thinking that he must be developing an ulcer. It was a bitch pulling over every day to puke his guts up on the side of the road, but he always ate a hearty meal around two in the afternoon and something light for dinner.

Selma would have a fit if he came home with some serious illness, just thinking about her pampering him made him smile and groan at the same time. She had a way about her that gave him comfort and happiness. He missed the brothers, but after his month and a half trip down memory lane, he was ready to settle into a new life and maybe find something to keep himself occupied with in his free time.

The Indian broke down in southern Ohio, and it took a few days to find the parts to fix the old bike, but eventually he'd gotten it repaired and was back on the road that same hour. Now he was an hour out of town and he slowed his speed. He knew in his heart that he'd done the right thing, but even with the peace he'd achieved during his mental health ride, his only regret would be the loss of the Bastards.

Selma's car was in the driveway when he turned onto their road. She must have had the day off. It didn't happen often, but he knew he had to face her, needed to talk about his ride and hope she wasn't too mad at him for being absent. He parked his sled next to her car and entered the house with his key.

She wasn't there, the place was empty once he searched it looking for her. Well so much for his dramatic entrance. He dropped his kit on the bedroom floor by the closet and headed for the shower.

Selma was at the hospital planning to visit Pressley after the tech finished sucking the blood from her arm through a huge needle. She watched the little tube fill with her blood and absently thought it was interesting that her blood was actually a dark purple. She had been lightheaded for a few days and ended up at the doctor's office this morning. He sent her over to the hospital for tests. The blood and urine samples would tell him what he needed to know and he always called in a day or two with the results.

She walked into Pressley's room and discovered Big Dog and Tiny were already visiting. Big Dog was reading a book out loud to the man in the bed, and Tiny frowned at her when she walked into the space interrupting the story. Since their little bitch session at the clubhouse, things had progressed to almost a friendly kind of truce. Thankfully, three days after she'd walked out, the huge man had come knocking on her door and they sat down and talked about her program.

She had made a few changes in her life in the past weeks, and she felt good about them. She had tendered her resignation to the County Board of Commissioners, and would be replaced as soon as the special election was put together to replace the sheriff, district attorney, and her position as a circuit court judge. She cited family needs as her reason for her resignation and although she caught flack from some people, she stayed firm.

Big Dog had been right. She was being a selfish bitch and her new plan of action would benefit the community and the MC. Charlie could keep his place in the family of bikers, and she would be fulfilled in her law career as well. Reopening a law practice would take some time to become self-sufficient, but she had time. The Bastards had a building that would work for her purposes. So far her plans were falling into place.

All that was left for her to do was to talk to Charlie, and if things set well with him, they could start planning that wedding he'd mentioned in his note. She hoped that his journey came to an end soon, she missed being held in his strong arms every night and waking up to his kisses each morning. Just thinking about his absence made her eyes water, and she had to switch her thoughts or she'd end up crying for no good reason.

"Hi, guys, how's Pressley doing today? I had to have some tests taken and thought I would stop in to see if there was any improvement before calling a cab to take me home. My car is at the garage and they just texted me that it is now in my driveway. So a lot of good it does me there, but at least it won't make me seasick to drive down the road with a broken shock in the rear end."

Tiny grinned at her. "Today is your lucky day then, we drove the van to town to pick up supplies and drop off a few things, so we can give you a ride." He looked to Big Dog to confirm, and got the nod. "See?"

She stood by Pressley's bed and noticed how slender the young man had become and reached for his hand to hold between her own hands. As she looked at his face, she saw his eyelids flutter, but no matter how close she looked they didn't open. "What do the doctors say? He looks so skinny lying here." She was talking more to him than the others in the room "Boy, when you wake up from your nap, you will be at the mercy of every female in the county trying to feed you. Charlie will drag you home with him and I'll fix pasta like you enjoy so much. If you eat your dinner I might even find some of my triple treat cookies, the last time I made them you and Charlie ate the entire batch, do you remember?"

Big Dog cleared his throat and Tiny acted like he didn't notice the tears sliding down her cheeks. So she laid the young biker's hand down next to his hip and leaned over him to give him a quick kiss on the forehead. "You rest and heal. I'll check back with you in a day or two." She walked around the bed and remembered her purse was on the nightstand. Turning to reach for it was a mistake. The room spun around her and she collapsed to the floor in a faint.

She woke up in the emergency room, with two smiling men and a female doctor that was issuing instructions to them for her care for the night. "Make certain she sees her doctor as soon as possible. When she wakes up," they noticed that she was awake and the doctor smiled at her as if she hadn't been interrupted just moments before.

"As I told your brothers, you need to stay off your feet, and you need to make an appointment to see your gynecologist as soon as possible. Pregnancy at your age is risky, and you will need to be monitored closely." She shook her head and smiled. "You must really want a baby to risk getting pregnant at this stage in your life. Good luck." The woman patted her shoulder and left the curtained cubicle, leaving her with the two grinning bikers staring at her.

"Did she just say baby?" Selma felt bewildered. She hadn't given a thought to birth control and had been having amazing sex with Charlie for... "Oh no, what will Charlie say about this?"

Her question went unanswered as the two laughed out loud and Tiny had to sit down in the lone chair to get his breath back.

Big Dog kept smiling as they waited for Tiny to bring the van to the door to pick them up. He said, "Don't worry, Charlie will be thrilled after he gets over the heart attack you are going to give him when you tell him. Look at me, Future is due in July, and after the idea sunk in, I am thrilled to pieces. Steven needs a sibling to boss around, and I always wanted a little girl to spoil, so if I can like the idea, Charlie can get used to it too."

He heard the vehicle outside and walked into the living room to see who had pulled up. He was surprised to see the Bastard's van parked at the curb, but what shocked him into moving was seeing Big Dog get out of the passenger side and open the back side door to reach in and carry Selma out of the vehicle. As they approached the door, Charlie flung it open and stood aside in concern while he waited for the big man to set her down.

Selma was telling him that she was fine and could walk, and Big Dog told her to button it. "The doctor said off your feet or didn't you hear that?" He turned to Charlie and handed her over into his arms.

"It's about time you got back. Church is at seven tomorrow night, don't be late."

The door shut behind him and the van pulled away from the curb before either of them spoke. They were too busy kissing and holding onto each other to speak coherently anyway. He made it to the bedroom and almost dropped her tripping over his kit on the floor but recovered and plopped his ass on the mattress with her landing hard on his stomach.

She was laughing and scooting off him as he gasped for breath. She cradled his face in her hands and kissed him gently on the lips. "I need to talk to you, before we go any further right now, would you get my purse off the floor in the living room? I heard it drop when you two He-Men insisted on carrying me like a sack of potatoes."

He sat up and looked at her for a minute. She looked good, if a little tired, but her cheeks were pink and her eyes were smiling. He nodded his head and groaned as he stood up and walked into the hallway toward the spot in the entranceway where her black leather purse sat on the floor. He hefted it and wondered what in the hell women kept in the damned things to make them so heavy. Hell, a man carried everything he needed in a couple of pockets. Women were strange, but he had to smile at her as he walked back into the bedroom. There were a lot of benefits to having a woman around.

"I don't know what's in this thing, but did you ever consider arm wrestling? As heavy as it is, you must have some good muscles in those delicate arms of yours."

She smiled and patted the bed next to her as she moved to open the snap under the flap of the bag. "I was just at the hospital to have some tests that my doctor wanted to run, and I peeked in on Pressley. That's where I ran into those two bossy funny men. I had a little faint and the next thing I knew I was waking up in the emergency room."

She rummaged around in her purse for a minute and handed him a black and white picture of what looked to him like a radar picture of a tornado. She looked at the picture as if she'd handed him a winning lottery ticket and he knew it must mean something important, but for the life of him he couldn't figure out what it was he held in his fingertips.

When he didn't say anything, he could see the frightened look cross her face almost like she wondered if he was happy or not. His next words reassured her that he had no idea what he held.

"Babydoll, I know this mean something, but for the life of me I can't figure out what you're trying to show me here. A little hint of something might be helpful, you know."

She put her finger on the small bean looking thing and pole axed him. "You see that little spot? That's our baby. I've been feeling off for a few weeks so I went to the doctor. They did this sonogram in the emergency room and… Oh God it never occurred to me to use birth control. I felt as dumb as could be when the doctor told me I was pregnant."

He stood and walked around the room twice. He looked at her and the picture still between his fingers, and walked around the room twice more. He stood in front of her and looked at her for long minutes before sinking to his knees and pushing her onto back. He pulled her slacks down enough to see her belly and roughly pushed the material of her blouse up to reveal her entire stomach area. His big hands laid over the exposed skin of her torso and he kept them there, staring at the smooth flesh beneath his touch. His lips kissed the spot between his splayed hands and he let his hands fall to her hips as he laid his head over the middle of her stomach.

"Do you know what you are? You are a miracle, woman, and I'll never be able to tell you how much I love you and what a gift you are to me. I never thought I would have a child of my own, but I never knew that you were waiting for me either. I don't have the words to make you understand and I might never have them." He lifted his head and locked her eyes with his. "I'll love you until I take my last breath, woman, never doubt it."

EPILOGUE

The wedding had been beautiful and Selma was thanking Future and Jolly for arranging the event on such short notice. She had shown Charlie her gift to him last night and he made slow sweet love to her afterward. The tattoo that she had snuck around to get Show to give her was simple and as she found out, the best present she could have given her husband. The words "Charlie's Heart" was now decorating the spot over the place where her own heart lay beating beneath the flesh and bones.

He was with the men doing their best to drain a keg of beer, and she felt sorry for him because it seemed the taste of beer gagged him nowadays. The scent of dryer sheets sent him running to the bathroom and he carried his sugar packet with him again. She bought them at the restaurant supply store to make certain he always had his favorite treat. No woman could be happier than she was and it was all due to the man that was looking back at her with his sexy smile.

ABOUT THE AUTHOR

RYDER DANE

I write about MC Groups aka Biker Books, because I've lived with Motorcycles my entire life. It made me smile when a reviewing reader said that there was a realistic feel to my writing! Having been an "Old Lady" since I was 19 gives me the advantage of using a few real details of MC life. I am very happy to bring readers my stories and having them invest in my characters' lives.

Website: Ryderdane.com

Books by Ryder Dane

Big Dog (Burning Bastards MC Book 1)
Nomad's Fall (Burning Bastards MC Book 2)
Charlie's Heart (Burning Bastards MC Series Book 3)

Sanctuary Within the Breed
(Lucifer's Breed MC Book 1)
Integrity Has No Bounds
(Lucifer's Breed Book 2)
Starting Over (Lucifer's Breed Book 3)